A Misfit Midwinter

December 1940

A Misfit Squadron Novella

Simon Brading

For James.

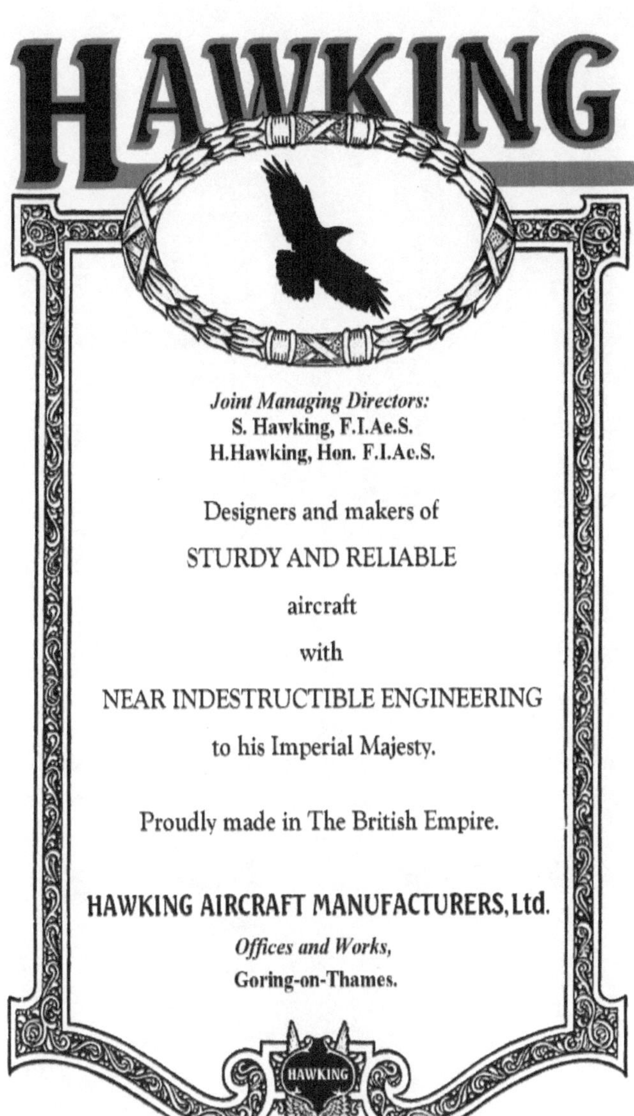
HAWKING

Joint Managing Directors:
S. Hawking, F.I.Ae.S.
H. Hawking, Hon. F.I.Ae.S.

Designers and makers of

STURDY AND RELIABLE

aircraft

with

NEAR INDESTRUCTIBLE ENGINEERING

to his Imperial Majesty.

Proudly made in The British Empire.

HAWKING AIRCRAFT MANUFACTURERS, Ltd.

Offices and Works,
Goring-on-Thames.

HAWKING
GORING-ON-THAMES

CHAPTER 1

Gwen Stone watched as Dragonfly, the aircraft of her commanding officer, Acting Group Captain Abby Lennox, was carried by the lift at the Arturo's bows into the hangar directly below the flight deck. The other five Misfit Squadron aircraft were already there and it was only her left in the air now. Because of the injury she had sustained when Wasp had been shot out from beneath her and the fact that she was in an unfamiliar aircraft, she had been instructed by Abby to wait until last before landing, in case of mishap.

'Badger Seven, this is Tinman. You are clear to land, repeat, clear to land.'

It took Gwen a second to realise that the carrier's radar controller was speaking to her; she wasn't only flying the incapacitated Mac's aircraft, Jaguar, for him, she had also taken his position in the order of battle. 'Tinman, Badger Seven here. Acknowledged, thank you.'

Gwen dropped out of her holding pattern and swung around to line Jaguar up on the aircraft carrier's stern.

She throttled back and Jaguar sank gently from the sky. A few twitches on the stick and rudder had the big twin-springed machine on the optimum flight path and she trimmed her until she would almost land herself if she let go of the controls.

Thirty seconds out and everything was perfect. It was time to put down her landing gear. She took her left hand off the throttle and reached for the gear lever. She gave it a tug, but it was stiff and she couldn't bring enough force to bear with her dislocated shoulder. With no other choice and no time left, she changed hands on the stick and reached across her body with her right arm.

Just as her fingers touched the lever, she was buffeted by a rogue crosswind coming off the cliffs of the coastline below and Jaguar swung perilously off course, her nose pointing at the sea instead of the metal deck.

Gwen fought the stick with her bad arm and stars flared to life behind her eyes as her shoulder protested, but she had no choice but to do it; her life depended on not losing control completely. Jaguar responded and levelled off quickly, but the damage was done - she was a long way off the glide path.

She had only moments to make a decision - throw on full power and abort, or trust in her ability and attempt to recover an approach that was looking increasingly lost.

Ordinarily, it would have been an easy decision to make; there wasn't a single pilot in the world, Gwen included, who, under normal circumstances, wouldn't have given up on such a disastrous landing attempt and gone around again. The only problem was they weren't normal circumstances; Jaguar was running extremely low on spring tension because of Gwen being last on the landing list and twin-springed aircraft didn't have the luxury of a reserve spring to fall back on.

To Gwen's mind there was only one option.

She rammed the gear lever home and switched her hands back over without waiting for the whirring from the small but powerful springs in the wing roots to begin. She immediately put the stick hard over to the left, setting Jaguar on her wing, then pulled back, banking hard. She stamped on the rudder pedals and threw on more power to keep the aircraft in the air, holding the extreme turn for a couple of heartbeats, then reversed it, throwing Jaguar through a full one hundred and eighty degrees and onto her opposite wing.

There was the aircraft carrier, almost directly above her from her perspective, far too close for comfort, and she pulled the stick into her lap again, banking towards it.

The man at the side of the deck who was responsible for helping pilots land was frantically waving his two red ping-pong bats at her to abort, but she blocked him out and focussed all her attention on where the arrester wires lay across the deck, waiting to a bring her to an abrupt halt.

Still turning, she crossed the stern of the aircraft carrier, her right wingtip only inches from it and wrenched the stick back to the left with both hands, gritting her teeth at the pain in her shoulder.

Jaguar responded beautifully. The aircraft that she, Mac, Abby and Kitty had designed together was incredibly agile despite its size and the wings came precisely level just as the wheels thumped hard into the deck. The hook under the big machine's tail snagged a wire, instantly jerking her to a standstill and throwing Gwen forward to be brought up hard by her straps. Burning agony shot through her shoulder once more and her eyes flickered closed as the pain overwhelmed her.

An insistent knocking on the canopy slowly brought her back to herself and she looked up to see Sergeant Jenkins, her fitter, standing on Jaguar's wing, peering through the glass in concern.

'You alright, Officer Stone?'

Gwen blinked at him, wondering how he had moved so quickly. 'Yes, fine. Yes. Thank you.' She thumbed the catches on either side of the cockpit and together they slid the canopy back on its runners.

'Would you shut down then, please, ma'am?'

Gwen lifted her gaze and saw that Jaguar's airscrews were still buzzing angrily. The big machine was straining against the arrester wire and it felt like she might break free at any moment. She cursed and reached across her body to pull both of the throttles back and lock them off, then grinned sheepishly at the fitter. 'Sorry.'

He chuckled, then leaned in to help Gwen with her straps. 'No problem, ma'am. It's not as if she's my machine anyway.'

Gwen grinned as she clambered awkwardly up onto the seat, but her legs were shaky beneath her and she grabbed at the edge of the cockpit to steady herself, idly wondering whether the carrier had gotten under way while she hadn't been looking

Jenkins frowned at her. 'Shall I get a medical orderly, ma'am?'

'No thank you, I don't want to make a fuss.' She forced a smile. 'I'll collapse when I'm not in full sight of the entire bloody Navy.' She tilted her head towards the observation pit running along the starboard side of the deck. It looked like most of the Arturo's off-duty crew had gathered to watch the Misfits return, despite temperatures being well below freezing. 'Just help me down, please.'

'Right you are, ma'am.'

Despite her increasingly unstable legs, Gwen made it to the deck in one piece. She nodded gratefully to Jenkins, who had managed to help her down without making it look like she needed him, but rather that he was just being gentlemanly. She gave a second nod to Jessica Hudson, Mac's fitter, who was anxiously waiting to take charge of her aircraft. 'Sorry for that landing.'

'Nothing to apologise for, ma'am.' The severe, black-haired woman said. 'She's down in one piece, that's all that matters.'

Gwen gave her a smile, then turned back to Jenkins. 'Would you accompany me, please? I'm not entirely sure I'll make it on my own.'

'It would be my pleasure, ma'am.'

'Thank you, Sergeant.'

They started towards the port side of the carrier, away from the watching naval personnel, heading for the nearest stairwell down to the hangar. Gwen managed to walk, held up mostly by her pride, but she was grateful for the presence of the fitter at her elbow; knowing he was there to catch her gave her strength. They only made it half way across the deck, though, before the lithe figure of Kitty came bounding up the stairs. She was still wearing her tightly-fitted red and white flightsuit and the way she looked in it as she jogged towards them took away what little breath Gwen had to spare.

'You alright, ma'am?'

Jenkins' whisper brought Gwen's attention to the fact that she had stopped walking in order to better appreciate the sight of the young woman. She felt her cheeks heat, even with the freezing wind blowing off the ocean. 'I'm fine. Just a bit... distracted.'

The fitter grinned. 'No idea why.' He nodded a greeting to Kitty as she bounced to a halt in front of them, grinning broadly, then turned back to his pilot. 'I'll leave you in better company than mine, then, ma'am. Take care of yourself; we need you to make another aircraft for us so we can beat that bugger Gruber for what he's done.'

'Will do, Sergeant, and thank you again.'

'Pleasure.' With a last nod, Jenkins wandered back towards Jaguar. He seemed almost at a loss for what to do, now that he didn't have an aircraft to take care of.

'So, how did Jaguar treat you? Was she upset at not being sworn at in a thick Scottish accent every five minutes? Or did she...?' Kitty broke off, her smile completely disappearing when she noticed the golden aircraft still sitting on the flight deck.

'What? What's wrong?' Gwen turned to see what the American was staring at and had to swallow to keep back the bile rising in her gullet.

The Misfit pilots had been trained to hit the third of four main arrester wires stretched across the deck of an aircraft carrier. That way there was no danger of them coming up short and missing the deck entirely and there was a spare wire in case they overshot. Gwen had managed to miss all four wires and been brought up by a fifth, a good few yards beyond, that was only there for emergencies. Not only that but, with how hard she'd landed, she'd been in real danger of bouncing over it and with her brief loss of consciousness she would most likely have ended up in the water off the bow.

'I've never seen you land so badly, are you...?' Kitty stopped when she saw Gwen's pallor and wrapped an arm around her. 'Come on, let's get you below.'

Gwen let herself be led towards the stairwell, leaning into the young woman more than was strictly necessary, but groaned and came to a halt again when Abby appeared from one of the stairwells towards the bow and strode towards them, her face like thunder. Gwen had hoped that she would have been too busy seeing to her aircraft to witness her absolute pig's ear of a landing, but no such luck.

'Gwen! What the hell was that?' The leader of the Misfits was already bawling even before she got even close to them. 'You should know better than to pull a stunt like that! If the wind pushes you off *bloody hell you look awful!*' Abby completely changed tack, her anger instantly disappearing to be replaced by worry when she got a good look at her pilot. 'For pity's sake, what are you standing around here in the cold for?'

Abby formed up on Gwen's other wing and together she and Kitty escorted her to the stairwell.

They made it almost all the way down to the hangar deck before Gwen's legs finally gave way and she could go no further. Rather than face the indignity of being carried, she called a halt so that she could rest and the two women helped her sit on the stairs.

'Stay here, I'm going for a medic.' Abby ran down the last few stairs and disappeared through the bulkhead door into the hangar.

After the engine room, the hangar was the most dangerous places on the ship, when not under enemy fire, at least, and there was always at least one medical orderly stationed there to cope with the all too frequent mishaps.

Kitty sat next to Gwen while they waited, as close as she could get without being on her lap. 'Is it just your shoulder or is your head hurting again?'

'I don't think it's my head, but everything's a bit fuzzy right now so I can't really tell.' Gwen reached up to undo her helmet, but Kitty batted her hands out of the way and did it for her, lifting it off to reveal the white bandages underneath. She laid the helmet, with its complicated array of lenses carefully to one side, before inspecting the back of Gwen's head. Thankfully, there was no sign of blood from the cut she had sustained only a couple of days before - the stitches had survived the flight and bumpy landing.

'My poor darling.' Kitty reached out to cup the side of Gwen's face and leaned forward to give her a gentle kiss.

'Yes, yes, that can wait. Stop canoodling and let me do my job, please.'

Kitty drew back with a start and the two pilots found a medical orderly standing at the bottom of the stairs smiling up at them. She was a pretty young woman, barely out of her teens, with fair hair and copious amounts of freckles across her cheeks and nose.

A grinning Abby was standing behind her. 'If you're well enough to behave like that, then I'm going to go back to bawling you out.'

Gwen grimaced. 'I'd rather you didn't; I've got a bit of a headache. Can't you just bawl out Mac instead? After all, it was his machine that almost landed me in the drink.'

The group captain chuckled, but shook her head. 'That's not going to fly, sorry. I will leave the dressing-down until you're better, though.'

'It's appreciated.'

'Excuse me!' The medic interrupted. 'Do you mind if I get my patient to sick bay? Or would you like me to go get you some tea and cakes while you finish your chat?' Whatever the young orderly might have lacked in experience she more than made up in authority and sass and, even though she softened her words with a smile, there was no mistaking the concern for her patient that prompted them.

Abby laughed. 'No, ma'am!'

She moved to help Gwen up, but Kitty waved her away with a smile. 'Don't worry, I'll take care of her. Without any "canoodling."'

Abby laughed. 'Thank you.' She looked at Gwen. 'I should get back to the hangar, but I *will* speak to you later.'

'Alright.' Gwen smiled feebly, not really looking forward to facing her commander, despite feeling that she had made the right decision.

CHAPTER 2

When Gwen and Kitty got to sick bay, Mac was already there, grumbling and complaining about being confined to bed.

He had protested vehemently that morning when Abby had ordered him to hand Jaguar over to Gwen. However, despite the fact that Gwen wasn't strictly fit to fly after she'd been shot down by Hans Gruber, the leader of the Crimson Barons, she was in better condition than Mac and it had either been that or leave the aircraft behind.

Mac had been carried by Dreadnought to the small airfield at a small town called Teriberka on the coast nearby, where the larger C flight aircraft were being dismantled for the journey, but the landing operations for A and B flights had taken so long that the naval personnel had had time to bring him out to the Arturo and make him comfortable before Gwen got there.

Kitty and the young orderly, who introduced herself as Polly Ames, got Gwen out of her flightsuit and into a hospital gown before putting her into the bed next to the Scotsman. Polly then excused herself, saying that she needed to get back to her station in the hangar. They thanked her and she nodded, giving them both a warm smile, before leaving Gwen in the care of the doctors.

Mac had watched the whole process, fidgeting, barely able to contain himself, and as soon as Gwen was settled he growled at them. 'Well? What did you do to my aircraft?'

Gwen briefly considered employing the usual Misfit modus operandi and teasing him by implying that she'd had some kind of accident, but then thought better of it; after the events of the day before, he likely wouldn't take it well. She smiled reassuringly. 'I had a rough landing and a bit of a fright, but Jaguar's in one piece, don't worry.'

Mac grunted and finally relaxed back onto his pillow. 'That's the last time I let a bloody Sassenach drive my bird.'

Kitty winked at Gwen before calling out to him in a sweet voice. 'What about a Yank? Or an Aussie? I hear Bruce wouldn't mind having a bit of a joyride in a fast aircraft...'

'No bloody way! If that numpty wants a ride in a decent machine he can build one hissel. Or fly *yers*.' Mac stabbed a finger at her to punctuate the word, then rolled onto his side, showing them his back.

Gwen and Kitty exchanged a dismayed look at the spite in Mac's voice; he had never spoken to his fellow pilots that way before and they wondered just how deeply the death of his beautiful Muscovite girlfriend, Katerina, had affected him.

Gwen was very quickly checked over by the efficient Navy doctors. They reassured her that the Muscovite doctors had done a good job patching her up and that the only thing that she could do was rest. They then released her, giving her willow bark pills for the pain and told her to go to bed.

Kitty was all for doing what the doctors ordered, saying that the other Misfits would most likely still be in the hangar taking care of their aircraft and Gwen agreed readily, but not for the same reasons as the American - all she felt up to doing was sleeping.

However, neither of them got their way because, no sooner had Gwen gotten into her nightshirt and climbed into bed, than Abby slipped into the room.

She asked Kitty to leave the two of them alone, then sat on the bed next to Gwen's and just stared at her.

Gwen was relieved to see that Abby wasn't angry anymore, but she still found that her mouth was dry; she had sorely disappointed her commander once before and hadn't ever wanted to again, but it seemed that she had.

'I...' she began, but Abby cut her off immediately.

'You had five percent tension left on your springs. Five. You should have diverted to Teriberka half an hour before you landed. They could have rewound Jaguar there and then one of the other pilots could have taken a boat out to pick her up easily. Trying to land with your injury wasn't worth the risk.'

Gwen nodded, afraid to say anything and Abby sighed.

'There's a stubborn streak in you which means that you often get a job done when anybody else would have given up long ago, but there's a big difference between plucky perseverance and downright bloody-mindedness and you need to know when to draw the line. You got away with it today, but you might not next time.' She shook her head. 'Look, I'm not expecting you to have learnt your lesson or anything daft like that, but I do hope you're aware that what you did was unnecessary and that maybe you'll think twice in future.'

Abby didn't wait for an answer, but just stood and went to the door. She turned around before opening it, though. 'Rest. You're off duty. I don't want to see you anywhere but that bed or the sofas next door for the next three days if it's not for meals. And no bloody thinking about the aircraft we're going to build you when we get back, alright?'

She grinned, then left before Gwen could reply.

As soon as Abby was gone, Kitty slipped back into the room.

'What did she say? Did she kick you out? Demote you back to an NCO? Please tell me it's that and I can start ordering you around; I'd quite like that.' Kitty winked lasciviously as she sat on the edge of Gwen's bed.

Ordinarily the American woman's clowning and overt sexuality would have Gwen laughing, but she found she couldn't quite summon the energy to do so. 'No, nothing like that. No punishment. But I'm starting to get the impression that I'm running out of second chances.'

Kitty waved away her words. 'Don't be silly. If you had any idea of the stupid things people like Mac, Bruce and Scarlet did while we were in France and got away with only a rap on the knuckles...'

'Then why is Abby making such a big thing of what I did?'

'Maybe it's because she cares more about you than the rest of us. You're special.'

It was Gwen's turn to wave away that notion as absurd. 'I really don't think so. Most of you are better pilots than I am. Or are you saying it's because I can design a few aircraft? Because, if you hadn't noticed, quite a few of you can do that too.'

'No, it's much more than just the skills you possess...' Kitty paused and shot a glance towards the door, as if to make sure that it was closed and nobody could hear her. 'Look, things in France got so fubar towards the end that tempers were flaring and we were almost fighting amongst ourselves. Then when Cece died we began falling apart as a squadron.' She shrugged. 'Any other squadron, a normal squadron, would just buckle down, stiffen that bloody British upper lip, fall back on discipline and keep going, but we can't do that. We barely have any discipline to speak of and we rely too much on *heart* to keep us fighting. And then when something breaks that heart...'

Gwen nodded; what Kitty was saying sounded all too familiar; her own broken heart had prompted her to join the RAC and throw herself into the war.

Kitty knew Gwen well enough that she knew exactly where her thoughts had gone and gave her a half smile before continuing. 'Anyway, since you joined, we've been more of a unit again, more like how we were in the beginning. It's probably as much to do with the circumstances as anything you're doing, but it's easy to see how Abby might think it was you who brought us back together and be protective of you.'

'That's silly.'

Kitty grinned. 'I know, right? But it's either that or she's in love with you too.'

Gwen laughed. 'Now that's *really* bloody silly.'

'Why? It's very easy to fall in love with you. In fact, I think I might have some competition.'

Gwen frowned. 'Who?'

'Polly, of course! Didn't you see how she was looking at you?'

'There might have been a bit of hero worship going on, I suppose.'

Kitty shook her head. 'Oh, no, it was much more than that, believe me.'

'Are you sure that she's... um... well... one of us?'

Kitty smirked. 'Us what?'

'You know, a woman who likes women.'

Kitty laughed. 'Is that what we are?'

Gwen scowled. 'I'm new to this, give me a break will you?'

'No way! It's too much fun to tease you.'

Gwen narrowed her eyes at her friend, but all she did was provoke more laughter so she turned her head away and pretended to sulk. 'I'm not sure I like women any more. Or at least one woman in particular.'

'Really?' Kitty reached out a hand to turn Gwen's head back, then held her gently in place while she bent forward.

Gwen looked up into the bright blue eyes of the woman who she had come to care for deeply over the last few months, feeling her tongue flick out to moisten her lips without her telling it to.

Kitty didn't kiss Gwen, though, but just hovered an inch away. 'I don't believe that for one second.' She chuckled gently, the sound sending Gwen's heart skipping, then closed the remaining distance.

For a few all too brief minutes, Gwen forgot all about her pain and worries.

They were still entwined when the thrum of the Arturo's idling engines deepened and the massive steel beast shifted as she turned, coming around to point her bow north, towards the open sea where the rest of the convoy accompanying her was waiting.

Shortly afterwards, they heard the door to the outer area of the rooms squeal open as the rest of the pilots arrived, their aircraft seen to.

Kitty gave Gwen a last kiss, then rolled gracefully off the bed and to her feet, just in time for Scarlet to burst in, followed more sedately by the rest of the female pilots.

Scarlet immediately marched over to Gwen's bed. 'I heard you had a bit of a turn. Are you feeling alright? You look flushed.' She glanced sideways at Kitty and gave her a crooked smile. 'So do you, actually. Maybe there's something going around.'

CHAPTER 3

Gwen managed to obey Abby's orders as far as rest was involved, sleeping until she was sick of it and getting up only to eat in the mess or snuggle up with Kitty on a sofa in the sitting room. What she couldn't do, though, was stop her mind from working and when Abby gave her permission to resume light duties on the third day she already had a fully developed aircraft in her mind.

Midshipman Simkin had once again been assigned to assist the Misfits and the young officer dug out some fresh paper and the other materials Gwen needed from the ship's stores, then showed her to a design room in the depths of the ship.

The Arturo had been conceived to be completely self-sufficient and had included such things as a hydroponic farm and a water treatment plant, as well as everything necessary to conceive and fabricate any spare parts or machines it might require during its voyage. Like most of those other facilities, the design room hadn't been used since the First Great War, but it was clean and perfect for her needs.

As soon as Simkin left her, Gwen pinned sheets of paper to the yellowing blotting boards of one of the rows of ornately carved wooden desks, then got down to work.

As always, the design in Gwen's mind evolved slightly while she was drawing it out, as if the process of transferring it onto paper allowed it take on a life of its own, but it was still done in a little under two hours and she rolled up her final blueprints, put them into the three-foot long cardboard document tube that Simkin had provided her with and started the long walk back up to the Misfits' quarters at the top of the ship.

The promised blizzard had set in only hours after the Arturo had set sail, bringing with it towering waves and high winds driving heavy snow. The flight deck was declared off-limits, which meant that the only views of the world outside available to most personnel were through the glass-covered portholes in the long access corridors ringing the ship. During bad weather, the crew had a curious tradition of going for strolls along those corridors, as if they were on a pleasure cruise, and Gwen passed dozens of off duty men and women, most of whom greeted her with a nod or a salute. There were even deck chairs in front of some of the larger windows where officers and ordinary ranks alike were snoozing or taking tea.

Gwen's route took her near sick bay and she came across Polly Ames and three friends, all women, on a break, watching the storm through a window.

The medic immediately looked Gwen up and down, assessing her, perhaps not entirely professionally. She had paid more than half a dozen visits to the Misfits' quarters over the last few days, ostensibly checking up on her patient despite the fact that Gwen wasn't strictly her patient and it had quickly become very clear that Kitty was correct that she was indeed "one of them" (Gwen still couldn't quite bring herself to use any of the other terms that were bandied about; in her eyes most of them were derogatory or downright insulting).

Polly nodded appreciatively. 'You're looking much better, even since last night.' She saw the tube in Gwen's hand and chuckled. 'You didn't waste much time getting back to work, did you? How long have you been off bed rest? Five minutes?'

Gwen shook her head. 'At least ten.'

Polly laughed, then turned to her friends. 'Ladies, this is Gwen Stone, one of the intrepid Misfits. Gwen, these are Betty, Rachel and Fiona.'

The girls nodded in turn and Gwen gave them each a warm smile. They were young, around Polly's age, fresh-faced and extremely wide-eyed at being in the presence of one of the legendary pilots.

Gwen blushed at the attention and looked away, but that only served to make her conscious of the fact that she was drawing quite a bit of attention from the other sailors in the corridor, many of whom were slowing in their wandering to stare, trying and failing to be surreptitious about it.

Suddenly uncomfortable and feeling the need to be anywhere but there, she gestured vaguely in the direction she had been going. 'Um, I should...'

Polly smiled kindly, already well aware of Gwen's view about being in the spotlight. 'Come on, I'll walk with you; make sure you don't get lost.' She linked her arm with Gwen's and drew her away, calling out to her friends over her shoulder with a smile. 'I'll see you guys at lunch!'

The girls looked very disappointed to be deprived of Gwen's company so soon, but called out their farewells and tittered excitedly amongst themselves when Gwen smiled and waved at them.

The young medic rolled her eyes at their behaviour, but waited until they were in a relatively quiet part of the corridor system before speaking. 'Sorry about that. They're very young.'

Gwen smiled, but didn't comment on the fact that Polly was their age, if not younger.

'So, are those the plans for your new aircraft?'

Gwen blinked and shot a glance at the girl. 'How do you know about that?'

Polly shrugged. 'Process of elimination - everybody knows you lost Wasp because we saw you land in Jaguar and we've all read Mr Featherstonehaugh's report about how you were shot down. Come and have a look.' She grabbed Gwen's hand, took her a short distance down an adjoining corridor and pulled her to a halt in front of a huge corkboard covering most of a bulkhead panel.

Among printed official notices and scribbled notes advertising social activities like musical groups, art tutorials and dramatic societies, were dozens of sheets of paper containing reproductions of the various articles that Freddy Featherstonehaugh, the journalist from The Times who had accompanied the Misfits to Vaenga, had transmitted to the British press over the last couple of months.

'Reading these helped keep us sane while we were stuck in Archangel with bugger all else to do except clear away ice and swab the decks. They were also the only way we had a clue what was going on with you Misfits because the officers weren't telling us anything, although I did get the impression they didn't know much more than we did.'

Freddy had given the Misfits copies of his reports and they'd read them with interest, but mixed feelings. They were funny and easy to read, but also provided an insight into the day to day struggle of the Misfits, not just with the enemy, but with their own doubts and fears.

Previously, the Misfits had always appeared in the papers as invincible heroes, but, without downplaying the importance of their actions, Freddy had made them into human beings, *people*, just like anybody else.

Gwen reread the article that dealt with the siege of Murmansk and described the loss of Wasp in detail, based on Abby's eyewitness account. Her vision blurred as she was once again overcome with sorrow at the death of her aircraft.

'I hadn't believed it before, but it's true, isn't it?'

Gwen was brought out of her misery by the softly voiced question and realised that, while she'd been reliving the past, the girl had been watching her. There was something between pity and sympathy in her expression which made her look a lot wiser than she should be for her age. 'What is?'

'That your aircraft mean more to you Misfits than they do normal pilots.'

Gwen forced a smile. 'Well, I think every pilot gets to know and love their aircraft.'

'Not like your squadron, they don't.'

Gwen considered, then nodded slowly. 'I suppose not.'

'It's because you put a lot of your own personality into them, right? You invest a lot, so if they get destroyed it's kind of like losing a part of you.'

Gwen stared at the woman, speechless, as once again she showed how perceptive she was. The tears that she thought she had banished came back in force and she swiped the back of her hand across her eyes to clear them then turned back to the board, uncomfortable under the girl's gaze.

She searched out the last of Freddy's articles. He had finished it the day before and they'd gotten a copy of it that morning, but she had been too busy with her work to read it yet and she wanted to see what he had said about the outcome of their mission.

The Misfits had been sent to Muscovy to hold back the Prussian forces and prevent them from taking the city of Murmansk and cutting off the northern supply route. They had been successful and the Prussians had been forced to retreat back into Finland to wait out the winter in safety, but just as the Misfits were heading to their rendezvous with the Arturo, hours before the weather had shut the airspace over the north for weeks, perhaps months, the Prussian bombers had struck. Where before the objective of their raids had been to weaken the defenders while leaving the city intact enough to use as a base, this time they took out their fury and impotence on its inhabitants, dropping thousands of bombs on the city, both explosive and incendiary, turning it into an inferno.

There had been no word from the city since, not a single message or signal and the Misfits feared the worst.

One of the biggest worries of Abby and Sky Commodore Dorothy Campbell, the officer in charge of the expedition, was that the public, and more importantly the King's ministers, would hear about the fate of the city and think that the entire mission had been a failure. Thankfully, though, Freddy had painted the Misfits' efforts very much as a victory, snatched under very difficult circumstances by valiant actions and sacrifice on the part of both the British and Muscovite pilots. At the request of the Tsar it made no mention of the betrayal of Polikasparov, the second in command of the Wolfpack Squadron, and Bruce's girlfriend, the Muscovite morale officer Natasha, but it did include the destruction of Murmansk, witnessed firsthand by the journalist from the transport aircraft taking him to the rendezvous. He'd had more time to watch the bombing than the Misfits, aided by optics lent to him by one of the fitters travelling with him, and his description of it was poetic, lamenting the loss of life, while at the same time raging against the reprehensible actions of the enemy at destroying an entire city filled with civilians. He ended by comparing it to the destruction wrought on the East End of London over the summer, something that would undoubtedly draw the sympathy of the British public.

However, none of that would stop the King's ministers, and especially the Minister for War, making what they would of the city's destruction.

Gwen turned away from the articles to find the girl still staring at her, rather too frankly for her liking. 'Thank you for showing me these, but I really do need to get back to quarters; Kitty will be wondering what I'm up to.'

The girl laughed. 'Does she keep you on that tight a leash?'

Gwen shook her head. 'I just meant that she'll be worried, you know, because I've been ill.'

'Ah.' The girl grinned knowingly and nodded. 'Of course.'

Gwen frowned at her; she got the impression that there was some meaning behind Polly's words, something that she didn't quite understand. She didn't want to ask, though, didn't want to extend their conversation any more than she had to, because while they had been standing at the corkboard the girl had been edging ever closer and now they were standing shoulder to shoulder, almost touching. 'Uh... I should...'

The girl nodded. 'Yes. You should.' She gave Gwen one last wide smile then took a very deliberate step back. 'But before I escort you home, why don't you take one of these?' She unpinned one of the papers from the board and handed it to Gwen. 'You and Kitty should come.'

Gwen perused the paper. It announced a "Meeting of Likes" that took place in the evenings of the first and third Saturdays of the month when not in port. She looked at the girl quizzically.

Polly shrugged. 'I can see you're still not comfortable with what you feel for Kitty. This is a group that we run for men and women like us.'

'I don't think...'

Gwen shook her head, about to refuse, but the girl cut her off. 'It will help you to see that we're just normal people and that there's nothing shameful in loving who you love.'

'I...'

Again the girl cut her off. 'Just think about it. Take the leaflet with you and discuss it with Kitty. It's more of a party than a meeting. Occasionally there are speakers and lectures, but mostly it's an excuse to eat and drink informally, surrounded by like-minded people.'

'Likes?'

The girl grinned. 'That's a kind of codeword. It's what people like *us* call ourselves when we don't want anybody knowing.'

Gwen blushed. 'Kitty told you about that?'

'She did, sorry.' The girl reached out and put her hand on Gwen's arm. 'It's very cute, but it's also very normal. We all went through the same thing as you at some point or other, but most of us didn't have an established community to help us or were lucky enough to fall in love with someone who thought the same way as us and was able to guide us.'

There was a brief flash of pain in the girl's eyes, but it was instantly gone as she drew back, replaced by her customary smile. 'Come on, let's get you home!'

They walked with the girl in companionable silence along a few more corridors and only a few minutes later found themselves at the door to the rooms assigned to the Misfits.

Gwen hesitated before turning the handle. 'Um... Would you like to come in and have a cup of tea?'

Polly smiled her thanks, but shook her head regretfully. 'I would really love to, but I go on duty in half an hour and I need to get ready. Perhaps another time?'

Gwen smiled. 'I look forward to it.'

'So do I and I'll see you tonight at the meeting!'

Before Gwen could say anything the girl beamed and skipped away. She greeted somebody she knew among the strolling sailors and fell into step with them, but glanced over her shoulder to give Gwen one last smile before disappearing around a bend in the corridor.

Gwen shook her head, exasperated as much at herself as at Polly's confidence that she would go to the meeting; she couldn't think of anything more uncomfortable or less British than talking about sexuality, especially one's own. For some reason, though, she found that she actually wanted to go.

She turned to go through the door, but stopped when she realised she still had the leaflet in her hand. She hastily hid it in a pocket of her work coveralls before entering the room, not particularly wanting any of her fellow pilots to see it and ask questions she didn't have an answer for.

The rooms were deserted, though, and silent except for the sound of heavy snoring coming from the men's dormitory.

Since he had been released the day after they had set sail, Mac had been spending a lot of time in bed. He had somehow managed to smuggle several bottles of vodka aboard from Vaenga and was very quickly working his way through them, something that had him unconscious much of the time and irritable the rest. The pilots were giving him a fair amount of leeway because of his injury and the death of his Muscovite girlfriend, but his behaviour was beginning to wear on nerves which were already frayed by the destruction of Murmansk and that the bad weather was only making worse.

Gwen didn't even consider disturbing him and just turned and went back out. She crossed the corridor, dodging around a group of wandering lieutenants, then went through the heavy bulkhead door into the stairwell and up to the hangar where she knew she would find the rest of her squadron.

CHAPTER 4

While Gwen had been on bed rest, the other Misfits had been working in the hangar, repairing their aircraft.

Not a single machine from A or B flight had escaped damage, but with stores running low at Vaenga, only those repairs essential to keeping the machines in the air had been done, so they were all in a very sorry state indeed. Every aircraft had at least one dull grey panel showing where a Duralumin panel had been replaced, but most also sported holes that hadn't been patched and what remained of their once pristine paintwork was scratched and pitted. Even Dragonfly, which had come through the battle over Britain completely unscathed, was looking the worse for wear and in the last desperate battle had gotten hit in the wing by a cannon round, which had torn a jagged hole through it, destroying one of her guns in the process.

With the storm looking to last until they were at least into the North Sea, there was no hurry to have the aircraft back in perfect condition, but the pilots were loath to leave them as they were and so had spent as much time as they could in the hangar. It wasn't so much a case of being ready to fly and fight if necessary, but rather, like Polly had rather astutely put it, that the aircraft were a part of their pilot - seeing them damaged or anything less than perfect *hurt*.

When Gwen came through the bulkhead door, her eyes automatically went to the bow end of the hangar, towards where Wasp had sat during the journey north, but of course her beloved aircraft wasn't there; she was lying in pieces at the bottom of the river that ran past Murmansk, along with hundreds of Prussian machines. She grimaced; no matter how many times she was reminded of the fact, or how recently, it still shot a sharp pain straight to her gut.

She put the lost aircraft out of her mind as best she could and picked her way carefully across the cavernous, but crowded space towards the three remaining A flight machines at the far end, making her way past the disassembled Dreadnought and B flight aircraft.

Each aircraft was surrounded by a group of people, some dressed in the dark blue work clothes of the Navy and some in the slighter lighter blue of the RAC fitters and pilots. The naval mechanics had been delighted to pitch in and help with the repairs, donating time that would otherwise have been passed idly, seeing as the two Navy *Martinet* fighters were grounded by the storm and didn't need working on.

Dreadnought was nearest to where she entered, at the rear of the hangar. She had been the most damaged of all the aircraft and had the most men and women swarming over her vast, disassembled structure. More than half of her Duralumin panels had already been stripped off of her frame and laid to one side and almost all of them would need to be replaced, but thankfully the Arturo carried more than enough spares in its stores to do so.

Beyond the immense aircraft was Dove, Chastity's white aircraft. She was a beautiful machine, twin-springed, with wings whose trailing edges curved gently and hadn't taken as much of a battering as many of the rest of the aircraft of B flight, mostly due to her pilot's brilliance.

Chastity had come to the squadron with very little in the way of mechanical know-how, unlike the rest of the pilots, but had pitched in with the repairs to Dreadnought on the journey to Murmansk, learning enough that she could at least carry out basic repairs on Dove and she was doing so now.

Next to Dove was Jaguar, her pilot conspicuously absent from the team working on her. Beyond her Derek was staring at the rear of Swift's fuselage, scratching his head over a large missing chunk of her horizontal stabiliser, which had only just been entirely replaced.

The last of the B flight machines, Hawk, was next to Swift and Kitty was straddling one of the two booms, wielding a paint brush. Somehow she sensed Gwen's presence and lifted her head to smile, giving her an enthusiastic wave and not noticing when she sprayed paint over the fitters surrounding the machine. Gwen laughed and waved back, but didn't stop to speak to her.

Hummingbird was the only one of the assembled machines that was still completely intact and only had one person working on her,

Scarlet, who was greasing her rotors and applying wax to her paintwork.

More than anything else it had been Scarlet's heroism in carrying out a daring, dangerous, but hilarious, raid on the Crimson Baron's airfield, destroying almost the entire Prussian complement of fighters, that had allowed the Misfits to do so much to hold back the enemy ground forces.

The storm had let up slightly the day before, allowing signals to get through and among the messages received had been one from St Petersburg. It informed the squadron that the Order of Tolstoy, the highest honour that could be bestowed on someone who wasn't a Muscovite combatant, had been awarded to four members of the squadron - Abby as the commander and top-scorer, Wendy, for the destruction she had wrought among the ground forces, Lord Drake, posthumously, for his valour and work training the Wolfpack pilots, and Scarlet for precisely that raid.

Just past Hummingbird were the three surviving turn fighters of A flight, lined up nose to tail. There were far more men and women working on them than any other machine, aside from Dreadnought, not because they were any more damaged, but rather so as to get them in full fighting form as soon as possible in case they were needed to defend the convoy.

Bruce and Monty were standing between their two identically-designed aircraft, deep in discussion, and Gwen nodded at them in passing, but kept going towards the last in line, Dragonfly, where Abby was supervising a team of fitters putting a freshly-shaped Duralumin panel in place on the wing.

She looked up as Gwen approached and smiled. 'You look like the Pied Piper.'

Gwen frowned, not understanding, but then, when Abby pointedly looked behind her, she turned and found that every single one of the Misfit pilots had followed her accompanied by most of the chief fitters and a few curious naval mechanics with nothing better to do.

Gwen blinked at them with wide eyes. 'What on *earth* do you all want?'

She tried to feign surprise and confusion, but the pilots weren't having any of it

'Look, you, we've been trying to look like we're working all morning, but really we've just been standing around waiting for you. It was taking you so long we were getting worried you'd fallen overboard, but now you're here just *get the damn plans out!*' Owen's comment brought a few laughs, but most of the men and women just stood silently, expectantly.

'Well... I'm not sure...'

'If you don't get those blueprints out right this second I'll throw you overboard myself.'

Abby's voice from right behind her made Gwen turn.

The woman had taken advantage of Gwen's attention being directed elsewhere to wheel over an empty tool bench, which just happened to be at hand for her to spread her papers out on. She positioned it between Gwen and the other pilots then went to stand with them, leaving her on her own, facing them as if a jury.

Gwen chuckled then popped the top off the tube and carefully pulled a large piece of paper out of it. She spread it out on the bench and, as one, the pilots and fitters moved forwards, craning their necks to get a better view. They said nothing, though; it was Abby's prerogative to ask the questions and she so after only a single glance. 'A gull wing? Interesting, but why?'

Gwen smiled at Abby's puzzlement. 'It's a good enough shape for the characteristics that we're looking for, but more importantly - look at the propeller.'

Abby frowned then looked back down at the plans. 'How the hell did I miss that? It's huge!'

'That's what *she* said...'

Bruce's quip earned him a guffaw from Scarlet and an elbow in the ribs from Owen and Gwen grinned at him before explaining herself. 'The gull wing puts the front of the fuselage higher off the ground, which allows for longer blades, so she'll be able to use the power of these new springs a bit better. It also means she'll be able to cope with better Ozzys or the Phoenix-type springs, whenever we get them.'

Abby nodded appreciatively. 'So she'll be damn fast and I can see she's manoeuvrable. What's this, though?' She tapped where the wings bent, angling gently upwards from the downwards sloping wing roots. There was some kind of mechanism between the two sections.

'Well, the wings are almost as large as Dove's so I reckoned that, if we're going to be travelling a bit and most likely on carriers, then I should do something to make her a bit more portable. I took advantage of the design to add a little bit of convenience - the wings fold upwards for storage.'

'That's a smart bet and a good solution.'

Abby looked around the members of her squadron, meeting their eyes, inviting them to comment, but none of them spoke, they just nodded one after another, so she turned back to Gwen. 'Well, the group approves and so do I. What are you going to call her?

'*Excalibur.*'

Abby frowned. 'Are you back to naming aircraft as weapons?'

Gwen shook her head with a smile. 'No, don't worry; I was just throwing a bit of a tantrum when I did that. Excalibur has always been a symbol for the British and it seemed quite apt; I conceived and designed it here, so in a way Gwenevere is borrowing Arthur's sword from him to wield in battle. It's also a good way to honour our friends here on the Arturo for getting us to Muscovy and back in safety.'

Approving murmurs sounded from around them at Gwen's words and proud smiles appeared on the faces of the naval fitters working nearby, who had clearly been eavesdropping.

Abby saw and raised her voice slightly, making sure that they could hear her. 'Well, we're not home yet and I'm not sure they deserve it, after trying to drown us on the way here...' She glared at them in mock anger and they hastily made their faces blank, pretending to be absorbed in their work, even as a couple of them nonchalantly wandered away to spread the news. She grinned, then turned back to Gwen. 'It's a very good name. I like it. However, I *am* worried about one thing.'

Gwen frowned and peered down at the plans, scanning them for something that she might have gotten wrong, even though she was sure there couldn't be anything. Finding nothing, she anxiously lifted her gaze back up to Abby. 'What?'

'Exactly *how* pink is she going to be?'

The pilots and crew laughed as Gwen sagged in relief and she grinned at them. 'Actually, I was thinking the same grey as the Arturo on top, with a black belly and only the wingtips in pink.'

'Good, then you won't have to do anything silly next time you decide to go gallivanting around at night.'

There were more chuckles at that; the bright pink of Wasp had almost gotten Gwen killed on a night interception, the moonlight reflecting off her paint and giving away her position. She had gotten over the problem by flying the aircraft upside down.

'Right then.' Abby clapped her hands and looked around at the group. 'It looks like we have a project to work on as soon as we get back. Now, if nobody has anything else to say?'

'Actually, before you all go.' Gwen spoke out. 'I'd like you to see something else.' She removed a second sheet of paper from the tube and laid it on top of the blueprints for Excalibur. 'While I was down in the design room I did this, too.'

Abby frowned at the second drawing. 'When you said you had ideas to improve Dragonfly, I wasn't expecting this... This is a major change.'

Gwen shook her head. 'Only the wings need to be completely replaced, the other changes are relatively minor, apart from the fuselage, but even that's only a case of extending the frame by six inches. The modifications shouldn't take more than five hundred man hours to complete. For a good team that's less than a week's work.'

'But she's almost unrecognisable!' Abby protested.

It was easy to see why she was upset with the changes Gwen wanted to make. Gone were the characteristic flared wings that made Dragonfly so distinctive and gave her the aspect of her namesake and in their place were something akin to gently swept bat wings. It was almost as if she were a whole new aircraft.

Gwen smiled apologetically. 'I'm sorry, but this feels right to me. Without starting from scratch, like with Excalibur, Sable or Raptor, I think this is the best way to keep Dragonfly ahead of the curve.'

Abby stared down at the plans, absorbing them.

Gwen and the other pilots watched her, collectively holding their breath, waiting to see what she would say and do.

Eventually she sighed. 'Oh, for pity's sake.' She looked up at Gwen. There was moisture in her eyes, but she still smiled. 'The design is brilliant, thank you.' She glanced over her shoulder. 'Sergeant Potter, come see what you make of these, please.'

Abby's chief fitter, Henry Potter, stepped out of the crowd and moved to Abby side. He peered down at the paper through his round glasses, scratching at the scar on his forehead from the head wound he'd suffered during the Prussian bombing of Badger Base a few months before.

He took a few moments to peruse them then looked up at his pilot. 'No problem, ma'am. We can do all that in a few days with the facilities here on the ship.' Mirroring Abby's gesture from before he glanced over his shoulder. 'Jack, come take a gander.'

The mechanic in charge of the hangar, Jack MacTavish, a grizzled man in his fifties who Gwen recognised as one of the tattoo artists who had given the crew their marks for crossing into the Arctic Circle on the voyage north, came forwards. He scratched his cheek while he peered at the plans thoughtfully, making a rasping noise that was audible even over the sounds of steam-powered tools and hammering coming from all around.

He almost immediately nodded. 'Aye, this'll be a cinch. Six days tops. Less if we get the boys and gals from the machine shop to give it priority.'

Both mechanics looked at Abby and she took a deep breath before nodding. 'One thing first, do you have a pencil, Gwen?'

Gwen handed her a drafting pencils and Abby bent over the blueprints. She made a few quick lines, then straightened up again. 'There we go.'

The entire squadron leaned forward to see what she had done to the blueprints, expecting some sweeping change to Gwen's plans that would keep the essence of Dragonfly. Instead, though, they just found five neat parallel lines through the last three letters of the aircraft's name in the bottom corner of the sheet of paper.

Abby smiled at them. 'If Dragonfly is going to evolve into something fiercer she's going to need a name to match.' She looked at Potter and MacTavish. '*Dragon* is all yours, gentlemen.'

The two mechanics grinned almost identical delighted grins, before nodding their acknowledgement.

Potter turned to Gwen and gestured to the plans. 'Ma'am? May I?'

Gwen gave her assent and he whisked them away, hurrying off to Dragonfly, Dragon now, with the naval mechanic, the two of them already deep in debate about how to proceed. The rest of the fitters and mechanics who had gathered to watch also drifted away, leaving only the pilots, who looked at Abby with not a little concern.

She just scowled at them, though. 'What the hell are you lot gawking at? Thanks to Stone here we've got even more work to do, so back to it! Come on! Chop chop!'

Once the pilots had wandered away, laughing among themselves, Abby let the scowl slip from her face. She sighed and turned back to Gwen.

She waved at the blueprints. 'I have to confess that I have no idea what the capabilities of this aircraft will be, it's so far beyond my design capabilities and imagination as to be laughable. Maybe Mac or Penny could make head or tail of her, but not me. What do you expect?'

'I'm projecting that it will be almost as fast as Hawk, but just as manoeuvrable as Sable or Raptor.

'Bloody hell...' Abby blinked in shock then peered down at the design, as if trying to decipher it. 'And how did you come up with this?'

'It's actually a concept that I've been playing with for quite some time, but there was always a piece missing.'

Gwen tapped the huge propeller and Abby nodded.

'Not enough power.'

'Correct. Excalibur reaches her best flying point around three hundred miles an hour. Previous springs wouldn't get her anywhere near that.'

Abby took one last long look at the plans then smiled wryly. 'Well, it looks like you've done it again. Now, why don't you put this away and pitch in with some of the extra work you've created for us. We need to get those modifications done if Dragon is going to have a hope in hell of keeping up with Excalibur.'

CHAPTER 5

Gwen bit her lip as she checked her reflection in the dormitory mirror for what must have been the fiftieth time. She didn't consider herself the best looking woman at the best of times and the RAC day uniform didn't exactly do much to help, but at least she was an officer now and the cut of her new uniform was rather more elegant than that of her old NCO one.

'Will you come *on*, already! We're going to be late!'

Gwen glanced over to where Kitty was leaning against the door jamb, tapping her foot impatiently.

It didn't seem to matter whether she was wearing full dress uniform or dirty work coveralls with a filthy face, Kitty was always beautiful. That night she looked particularly good because she had actually made a bit of an effort, pressing and starching her uniform and, despite regulations (which the Misfits largely ignored), her hair was down, spilling over her shoulders in a golden cascade.

All of which just served to make Gwen feel worse about her own appearance.

As if sensing her thoughts, Kitty pushed herself away from the wall and strode over on long, lithe legs. She grabbed Gwen by the shoulders, turning her to face her, then bent forwards to press their lips together.

Gwen found herself melting in the woman's strong arms, feeling as if her legs would give way beneath her if Kitty let her go. All too soon, though, the woman was pulling back and Gwen reopened eyes which had closed involuntarily to find Kitty smiling down at her.

'You're beautiful, Gwen. Never forget that.'

It was a good few seconds before she could recover enough presence of mind to get her feet back under her and she gave Kitty a disapproving frown when she caught sight of her rumpled clothing and smeared lipstick in the mirror.

'And you're incorrigible.'

Kitty laughed, then reached out to use her thumb to wipe away the smudges on Gwen's face. Her own makeup, of course, was still perfect, probably the result of the American cosmetics she wore. 'There, good as new. Now, stop fretting and let's get a damn move on!'

She dragged Gwen away from the mirror and out of the room.

'You came!'

Gwen and Kitty were barely through the door before they were confronted by a squealing Polly, who had obviously been keeping an eye out for them. She disengaged herself from the group of people she was speaking to, one of dozens filling the space, and bounded towards them, drawing the attention of every person in the room. She hugged them in turn, then grabbed them both by the hand.

'Come and meet my friends!'

Gwen was all too conscious of the eyes that followed them as the girl all but dragged them across the moderately-sized recreation room where the meeting-cum-party was being held. She looked across at Kitty, wondering how she was taking it and was not surprised to see that the American was completely unperturbed and smiling broadly.

Gwen was, however, surprised when she saw a very familiar face among Polly's group and couldn't stop herself showing it. 'Mr Simkin!'

Polly immediately tutted, her eyes glinting over her smile. 'No ranks or surnames, please, ladies. We're all on a first name basis here.'

Gwen blushed slightly. 'Sorry!'

'No matter; you weren't to know.' The girl shook her head, then waved at the young Midshipman, who blushed and gave them a shy nod. 'You've already met Billy, and these are Archie, Regina, Tabatha and Nancy. Guys, this is Gwen and Kitty.'

As soon as the introductions were done Polly smoothly took the conversation back to where she and the group had left off. Of all things they were talking about *cricket*, something that Gwen didn't know too much about or liked very much. Thankfully, rather than discussing the sport itself, they were debating whether nations who didn't play it were more aggressive as a result, with Archie and Billy Simkin citing the problems with Prussia during the previous half century as conclusive proof.

Bruce would have been horrified at the way his beloved sport was being discussed with complete disregard for the game itself, but Gwen found herself laughing at the ridiculous yet credible arguments put forwards, both for and against, while simultaneously impressed by how convincing the men and women made them, betraying both their intellect and sense of humour.

The conversation evolved naturally onto other subjects, as all conversations do, but even though they never approached anything unseemly or unacceptable in polite society, Gwen found herself becoming more and more uncomfortable. After about half an hour, she excused herself, pleading thirst, then grabbed Kitty's arm and pulled her away towards the buffet table next to the entrance.

They stood with their backs to the table, surveying the activity in the room, sipping at Kvass and nibbling on small pieces of toast covered with caviar, which Gwen had developed a taste for in Muscovy simply because it had been the only thing without beetroot in it.

Gwen frowned, unable to find the source of her unease.

Kitty saw her expression and grinned. 'Not quite what you were expecting?'

Gwen shook her head. 'Not in the slightest.'

'So what *were* you expecting?'

'Well, not something this *normal*, that's for sure.' Gwen smiled wryly when Kitty laughed. 'At university there was an amateur theatre society and the members, mostly male, were always in the union, pawing at each other while they drank. They seemed to be trying to outdo each other with how camp they could be, calling each other "ducky" and "darling", and being overtly... well, *you know*.'

Kitty laughed. 'They're theatricals, they're obliged to act like that, no matter their preferences! And as for their overt sexuality,' she shrugged, 'some of us are like that, but most aren't.'

'That's a relief!' Gwen grinned, but then she became serious. She put her drink on the table and turned to face Kitty. 'Right, then, now that I'm here and any chance I have at keeping this a secret is well and truly gone, what *do* we call ourselves? I know what *other* people call us, but I hate those names. So, tell me, what is acceptable to us? That name Polly has on her leaflet? "Likes"? That feels a bit awkward to me.'

'Well, look at you all serious, ducky!'

Kitty pouted and flounced, laying her hand on Gwen's arm, then laughed at the sour expression she received in return. 'Sorry, couldn't resist, and no, "likes" is just a codeword that we all understand, but few people use. *Homosexual* is safe, but it's a bit clinical. I personally prefer *lesbian*, which has its origins in an ancient Greek poet, Sappho, who lived on the island of Lesbos, but most people use *gay*, because it can refer to both men and women. And besides, it just sounds happy, right?'

'I suppose.' Gwen considered the words.

She hadn't come across most of them before; homosexuality wasn't really spoken about in Britain, but then again neither was any kind of sexuality, it was just accepted as existing, then left for the privacy of the bedroom. Unfortunately, some countries weren't so tolerant and homosexuals were insulted, or worse, accused of being unnatural and persecuted.

'I think I like lesbian best, but I don't mind gay; you're right, it does make us sound like happy people.'

'Lesbian it is then!' Kitty chuckled.

They both looked up as the door next to them opened and were startled when the captain, Johnathan Hewer slipped in, surprisingly unobtrusively for such a big man. He saw them and moved over to join them, grinning widely among his copious facial hair.

'Evening, Captain.' Gwen said with a nod, then grimaced when Kitty rolled her eyes at her. 'Oops, sorry.'

The captain laughed, a low belly-rumbling noise. 'No matter! Gwen, isn't it? And, sorry, I want to say Katherine, but...'

'Kitty.'

'And you can call me Johnathan.' He fixed himself a drink, downed it, poured another, then nursed it as he looked around the room. 'Good turn out.' He nodded appreciatively, then turned back to them. 'Are you enjoying yourselves?'

Gwen nodded. 'We are, uh, Johnathan. We're just taking a bit of a breather to get some refreshments.'

'Good, good.' He smiled knowingly and tilted his head towards the mingling men and women. 'They can be a bit overwhelming sometimes, which is why I always try to be fashionably late, but they're good people if you give them a chance.'

'Oh, it's not that!' protested Gwen. 'I'm just... well...'

Kitty put her arm around Gwen, coming to her rescue. 'Gwen here is still a little bit new to our little world.'

'Ah, I see.' The captain nodded in understanding.

'And you?' Gwen asked, curious despite herself. 'Are you a part of... this?' She waved her hand vaguely.

The captain chuckled and glanced at Kitty. 'You weren't joking when you said she was new!' He looked back at Gwen. 'As captain I am responsible for the entire crew. I would show my face at this and any such gathering on my ship to let them know that they have my approval, no matter my own leanings.' He grinned at her, a twinkle in his eye. 'However, some such gatherings are much more to my liking than others.'

He saluted them with his drink then sauntered off, putting a slight sway to his hips that wasn't usually there and winking at them over his shoulder.

Gwen laughed in delight and was amazed to find that all her doubts about her love for a woman had been completely dispelled by the ludicrous sight of the captain of such a powerful ship being so open about his tastes and not a little effeminate, especially after the powerful spectacle he had provided as the Lord of the Winter Sea on the voyage to Muscovy.

She turned to Kitty and stood on tiptoes to plant a quick kiss on her girlfriend's lips. 'Come on, I want to mingle a bit.'

Kitty blinked at her in surprise, then smiled. 'Sounds good to me.' She wrapped her arm around Gwen's waist and pulled her close as they went back to the party.

After an hour of casual conversation, everybody grabbed a folding chair from a stack in an adjacent store room and sat down to listen to a couple of informal talks. Both talks were presented with humour by their exponents, but one of them, an absurd monologue on the correct choice of under clothes for the first night with a new lover, illustrated by examples of the mistakes that the woman in question had herself made, had the people in stitches.

After the talks, more food was brought out, along with tin mess plates and the people were encouraged to wander around, speaking to people they didn't know.

Polly separated Gwen and Kitty with a smile, explaining that it was intimidating enough to try to speak to one hero, let alone two of them at the same time, but even then, for a while nobody approached Gwen. She was feeling much more comfortable, though, and after she had introduced herself to a few men and women she was all but swamped by people wanting to get to know her. Rationally she knew that it was because she was a Misfit, but a part of her wanted to think that Kitty had been telling the truth and she was a little bit attractive.

The meeting finally broke up just before midnight, in plenty of time for the change of watch and the two Misfit pilots bid Polly goodnight, thanked her for such an enjoyable time and wandered towards their billet.

Gwen smiled contentedly as she and Kitty walked arm in arm. She was tired but very happy that they had gone and more sure of herself than she had been in months.

CHAPTER 6

The men and women of the machine shop worked around the clock to adjust Dragon's frame, reshape her panels and produce her new wings. As predicted by the naval mechanic, Jack MacTavish, the modifications were finished in just under five days, however, a full test was needed before she could be pronounced airworthy. Unfortunately, there was no chance for her to fly because the weather continued to be far too bad.

During that time, the convoy forged on homewards, barely seeming to make any progress against waves that seemed almost as tall as the Brunel Tower of Buckingham Palace. The Misfits were extremely glad to be aboard the Arturo, because the immense ship was barely moved by the sea's fury, even at the height of the storm, but Dorothy Campbell and Freddy Featherstonehaugh, travelling in the flagship, reported that even some of the most experienced sailors were having trouble keeping their food down in the smaller ships. However, even if the Arturo had been pitching and rolling like the other ships, it was unlikely that the Misfits would have noticed, so engrossed were they with their own machines and the new project. Mac finally surfaced as well, although he didn't do much in the way of work, which was just as well, because he was never very far from a bottle.

Finally, after eight days of driving snow and gales, the clouds parted and the winds calmed. Even though there were only a couple of hours before dark, none of the Misfits or the mechanics wanted to miss out on the chance of seeing what Dragon could do and permission was obtained from the captain for Abby to test her. However, as luck would have it, just as she was putting on her flightsuit, a priority message arrived for her.

Badgers to Smoke, however possible and with all haste. George R.

The message was easy enough to decipher. George R was the King, of course, and London had garnered many nicknames over the years, but the one that had been most appropriate and had stuck, even after most coal fires in the city had been replaced by gas, was that of "The Old Smoke". It had been adopted by the war office as the codeword for the capital in coded communications. Also the way it had asked for "Badgers" and not "Badger Squadron" was fairly clear - for some reason it was the pilots who were needed, not their aircraft.

What was of most concern to Abby, though, was the part of the message that read "however possible and with all haste". It spoke of an urgency that was going to be hard, if not impossible, to carry out and she immediately abandoned all thoughts of a joyride in Dragon and rushed to the bridge to speak with the captain. He was already aware of the contents of the message, though, and was deep in discussion with his first officer, Commander Twining, about how to best obey the order.

They quickly, but reluctantly, came to the conclusion that there was only one way to carry out the orders; the smaller Misfit aircraft were well out of range of the British Isles and would be for days, so there was nothing for it but to leave them behind and go in Dreadnought, the only aircraft that could make it and had the capacity to take all the pilots. However, even the big aircraft would be hard-pressed to reach British territory and the Arturo was going to need to close the distance somewhat before she took off. That meant abandoning its relatively safe course to Iceland and steaming directly for home, perilously close to Norway and waters that were Prussian-controlled and likely infested with undersea boats.

So, only fifteen minutes after the telegraph machine had stopped chattering, the Arturo, along with three agile and heavily-armed obliteration-class escort ships, broke off from the main convoy, stoked their boilers and steamed at full speed directly for Britain. At the same time, the process of swaying the separate pieces of the newly-repaired Dreadnought through the side bulkheads and up to the flight deck using the waist cranes was begun and the entire complement of Misfit fitters and Navy mechanics raced to assemble her.

While all that was going on, the pilots packed, readying to leave the Arturo for the last time. Due to restrictions on weight and space, they couldn't take everything with them, so they put some essentials in a kitbag along with their dress uniforms and gave the rest to Mister Simkin to be stowed and transported with their aircraft to wherever the Misfits ended up, which would most likely be Bagshot Hall, unless the King had other orders for them.

Polly had heard about the message through the ships scuttlebutt and she came by to say goodbye to Gwen and Kitty, embracing them both warmly and shedding a small tear. They promised to write and to meet up whenever their respective leaves coincided, but all three knew that it was more than likely that they wouldn't see each other again until the war was done and dusted.

It was the second time that the mechanics had assembled Dreadnought on the flight deck and, even though they were doing it at night, they pulled out all the stops and had her airworthy in record time, several hours before dawn. Getting the Misfits on board and settled in took less than ten minutes and then she inflated her balloon and floated into the sky, watched by almost the entire crew. It was a tranquil beginning to an extremely nervous four-hour flight at top speed and in the dark across more than a thousand miles of open water to a small airfield in the extreme north-east of Scotland, where she stopped only briefly to refill her hydrogen tanks before continuing the flight.

After slightly more than six hours, just after eleven in the morning, Dreadnought entered London's airspace. She was given priority landing clearance and was directed to the Royal hangar at Hyde Airstrip, where a frantic Royal Guard captain urged the pilots to change into full dress uniform as quickly as they could, before bundling them into three waiting autocars. They were then taken at breakneck speed through the streets of London, careening perilously around Trafalgar Square, then zoomed along Whitehall at several times the legal limit. The drivers didn't slow down when they reached their destination, either, and the wheels of the heavy machines almost left the ground as they hit the steep ramp down into the basement autocar bay of the Palace of Westminster. They raced around the claustrophobic space, barely dodging reinforced concrete columns and the small spring-powered vehicles of the ministers, before finally screeching to a halt at the doors of a pneumatic lift.

The lift was only just big enough to accommodate the pilots and their guide and took them up into the Palace itself, the doors opening into a short, wood-panelled corridor that led only to a private, well-appointed lounge where refreshments were waiting for them. There, the guard captain told to wait, then slipped out of the door into the main chambers, leaving them alone.

After all the frantic rushing around the sudden inactivity was surprising, to say the least, but they were in the military, so they were used to such hurry up and wait behaviour on the part of their superiors.

The bacon sarnies the mess of the Arturo had provide them with had run out fairly quickly during the flight and most of the pilots were hungry, so they dived straight onto the sandwiches and pastries provided and made an attempt at draining the large brass tea urn ticking away cheerfully in the corner of the room. Mac left the tea alone, though, and just swigged from the hip flask, which was all he could conceal in his dress uniform, while he picked at a croissant.

Almost half an hour went by before the door into the Palace opened again and the Misfits looked up, expecting it to be the guard or perhaps someone like the Marshal of the Court, however, the woman who appeared was dressed like them in an RAC uniform.

'Penny!' Abby led the rush and, heedless of both their uniforms, threw her arms around the woman, folding her into a hug that was crushing enough to overcome the resistance of the dozen or so petticoats between them.

'Abby, dearest.' Penny returned the hug, a single tear of joy escaping eyes that were squeezed tightly shut.

When Abby finally relaxed her hold enough that Penny could breathe again, she opened her eyes and smiled at the rest of the squadron. 'Hello, darling Misfits. I'm so happy to see that you all made it back in one piece!'

The pilots began to fire a barrage of questions at her and she laughed and held up her hands. 'Hold your horses!' When the Misfits quietened again, she shook her head and smiled enigmatically. 'Let me just get myself a cup of tea, then I can answer all of your questions.'

She walked to the brass urn, where she bent to fill a cup, added milk and sugar, then turned and walked back.

The simple act of crossing the room and pouring oneself a drink was unremarkable and would have brought no comment if carried out by anyone else, but Lady Penelope Bagshot had lost both of her legs only a few months previously and the ease with which she accomplished the feat was astounding. Especially seeing as the last time they'd seen her, she'd been staggering around like a newborn foal. Now, though, there was barely any sign that she had been injured.

She came to a halt in front of them, perfectly steadily, and grinned at them over the rim of the delicate Wedgwood cup.

Again the torrent of questions broke over her, but she remained impassive in the face of them and merely raised an aristocratic eyebrow at Abby.

Abby shushed her pilots. 'Settle down, everyone! Let the poor woman find her feet!'

There was a sudden stunned silence as the Misfits stared at their commander, aghast.

Lady Penelope just snorted, though, all pretence at ladylike behaviour lost as tea came out of her nose and she broke down into guffaws. When she finally managed to calm down again, she dabbed at her eyes then nose with a handkerchief that she produced from her sleeve. 'Oh, thank you, Abigail. I needed that.' She glance around the Misfits, who were still uncertain as to what to do and sniggered. 'Everyone's been pussyfooting around me far too much since my accident and I have been getting well and truly fed up.'

'I'm sure that nobody in this squadron would *ever* be anything less than totally frank with one of their own.' Abby gave her pilots a pointed look and they all had the decency to look slightly ashamed.

'Thank you.' Penny nodded gratefully. 'Now, while I've got this walking lark down pat, it *is* a bit of an effort to stand still so, if you don't mind, I'm going to plonk myself down.'

She flopped heavily into the nearest armchair and looked up at them while going back to sipping her tea.

When she was settled, Abby asked her what was on everyone's mind. 'Have you got any idea why we've been rushed here so urgently? Seven hours ago we were a couple of thousand miles away in the middle of the ocean!'

'Gracious! You really did hotfoot it to get here on time, didn't you?'

'Get here for what, Penny?'

Abby was running out of patience and pressed her friend, but Penny wasn't offended. She did, however, shrug. 'I'm sorry, I have no idea, but I suspect we're about to find out.'

She nodded towards the door, which had just opened to admit the same Royal Guard who had brought them to the Palace.

He gave them a nod and spoke quietly but firmly. 'Would you accompany me please?'

It seemed that once more they were in a hurry and he chivvied them out of the room, then marched them quite rapidly down thickly carpeted hallways with impressive portraits on the walls.

The hallways and corridors were completely deserted, apart from a few clerks who barely looked up as they passed, and they made it to their destination in quick time, but then, infuriatingly, they were told to wait again while the captain slipped through a thick wooden door.

Thankfully, it was less than a minute before he came back and beckoned urgently for them to go in. 'Single file, go down to the front row of seats as quietly as you can and file along until you fill them. Do not sit until the King gives you the wink.'

Gwen had never been to the House of Parliament before so she had no more idea of where they were or what they were doing than when they had arrived. However, she assumed that they were about to find out, so she held her tongue and her back straight as she followed the rest of the Misfits into the room beyond the door.

She could tell right away from the quality of the sound in the chamber beyond that it was large, but she was in no way prepared for what she encountered.

The door opened up onto a balcony with a dozen rows of tiered seats, like in a theatre, but it was what they overlooked that caused a hitch in her steps.

This was where the King and his ministers met to discuss policy, the place where laws were passed and decisions were made that affected a fair portion of the world.

Down below her, a couple of hundred men and women, dressed in black, occupied blue leather benches in two opposing groups on either side of a long and ancient-looking table. Between them, near the head of the table, sat the King on an ornate, high-backed wooden chair that didn't quite reach throne status. His position in the room was as much symbolic as practical - he formed part of neither side and, while his was the ultimate word, any decisions he made were made under the gaze and, theoretically, the approval of the representatives of the people.

Or at least that was the theory.

In practice it was very different. The ministers never really cared much for representing the people who had voted for them and were always trying to snatch as much power for themselves as they could. Up until that point they had been unsuccessful, but they had been able to use the excuse of the defeat in France to take away some of the King's autonomy, saddling him with one of their own, Regis Cummerbund, as a Minister for War.

Technically, the minister's job was solely to advise while the King continued to make the decisions. However, a precedent had been set and, even though Cummerbund had proved to have widely different opinions to the King as to how to run the war, especially where the Misfits were concerned, the King couldn't afford to ignore him completely otherwise, if there were any further defeats, he could well find himself losing more than just command over the armed forces.

It was that man, Mr Regis Reginald Rufus Cummerbund, who had just begun to speak when the Misfits entered the chamber, his voice clear and loud despite his advancing age.

'Your Majesty, distinguished colleagues, thank you for allowing me this opportunity to address you as regards the progress of the war with the Prussian Empire.' He bowed his head to the King to show his respect, but it was a minute gesture that was barely perceptible. 'It is with a heavy heart that I am obliged to report that the situation is increasingly dire with each passing day, indeed each passing hour. Quite aside from the setbacks we are facing in North Africa and the Mediterranean, the convoys bringing desperately needed supplies, purchased at great expense from our friends across the Atlantic I might add, are being intercepted and destroyed. This, as we all we know, means that resources are becoming increasingly scarce.'

He paused for effect and glanced around the chamber, meeting the eyes of the men and women grouped around him one by one, before his gaze finally coming to rest on the King, where it remained during his next words. 'It is time to tighten our belts and stop wasting what little resources we have on frivolous endeavours.'

He paused again, still looking at the King, forcing his point across, before looking down at his papers.

'I believe the experiment, started by His...' Cummerbund's eyes came up from his speech and he stopped in mid-sentence as he finally noticed the row of pilots standing directly in front and above him and blinked in surprise at men and women who by all rights should have been thousands of miles away.

Up until that moment, the attention of everyone in the room had been firmly fixed on him, but now, as silence filled the chamber, every eye turned to see what he was staring at.

The transition from silence, to eager murmuring, to thunderous applause, took all of three heartbeats.

CHAPTER 7

Gwen stood at the wooden guard rail as the noise washed over her. While the applause from the ministers in the chamber below was enthusiastic and polite, the public in the gallery ringing it were far more rowdy, as many of them added their voices or even whistled to show their approval.

She took it all in with a single scan, sweeping the room just as she did the sky, seeing expressions ranging from awe, pride and delight on the faces of everyone, politicians and civilians alike.

Except for two people.

Two people in the entire chamber reacted very differently to the appearance of the Misfits. One was the man standing at the table in the centre of the room - Cummerbund. His surprise had swiftly changed to anger at seeing the Misfits, his face darkening to a most unbecoming shade of red. He had managed to control himself after a couple of seconds, though, and regained his politician's mask, but Gwen couldn't help but chuckle when he glanced around surreptitiously, trying to see if anybody had noticed his lapse.

Nobody had, apart for Gwen and the one other person down below who hadn't joined in the cheering.

Throughout the uproar, the King had sat in his chair, leaning back and smiling faintly, his eyes fixed firmly on the Minister for War and it was only when the man reluctantly started to clap that his smile widened and he joined in with the applause himself. He allowed the noise to go on for few seconds more, but then he looked up at the Misfits and gave them a big grin, along with a wink and a nod. As signals went it was fairly obvious and would have given away the fact that the interruption had been planned, but fortunately nobody was watching the King so they didn't notice

The Misfits sat, but it took a good few seconds more for silence to fall completely and the people to take their seats once more, but then their gaze returned to the man in the centre of the room.

Cummerbund looked around, as if surprised to be the centre of attention once more and for a while it seemed like he didn't quite know how to proceed. He peered down at the papers with his speech for a few seconds, but then just gathered them up, folded them in half lengthwise and put them into the inside pocket of his long-tailed suit jacket. He took a deep breath as if steeling himself, then cleared his throat and resumed speaking.

'Your Majesty, distinguished colleagues, as I was saying before we were so pleasantly interrupted...'

The Minister for War's speech was rambling, lasted more than half an hour long and sent half the already-exhausted Misfits to sleep. It dealt mostly with logistics and the need for continued rationing and care with resources, but contained nothing that directly affected the squadron. This puzzled the Misfits somewhat and naturally was the only subject of conversation when they were taken back to the lounge and were again told to wait.

'Did you see his face when we showed up?' asked Gwen, looking around the group. When they shook their heads she grinned. 'You could almost see what he was thinking. Something like "bloody hell, I can't make this speech after those blighters have gotten *this* reception!"'

Abby nodded. 'So, you think he was going to use his speech to continue his agenda against the King and us?'

'Indeed, that was exactly what he was going to do.'

The voice came from the doorway and the Misfits leapt to their feet as the King strode in, grinning from ear to ear, followed by the Marshal of the Court and the guard captain.

'Morning all! Please, remain seated!' He wandered over to an empty armchair next to Abby and settled into it with a sigh, squirming slightly. 'That bloody chair down there might look impressive but it's dashed uncomfortable.' He looked around at the group. 'First things first, welcome home and bloody good job, bloody well done!'

'Thank you, sir.' Abby answered for her squadron, but they all beamed, pleased by the King's approval.

'Now, before we talk about why I had you "hauling arse", as the Americans put it so quaintly,' he nodded at Kitty, who raised her teacup at him in salute, 'I have a few admin things to do.' He held his hand over his shoulder and the Marshal of the Court stepped forward to hand him a piece of paper. 'I've got some gongs to hand out and Sir Douglas has very kindly given me special permission to inform those of you who've earned promotions by your deeds in Muscovy, basically because I ordered him to.' He glanced at Scarlet, who had sat up straight at the name of her boyfriend. 'He sends his love, by the way and says he will see you this evening at the Ritz.'

Scarlet all but bounced up and down in her chair at the news. 'Thank you, Your Majesty!'

The King laughed at her enthusiasm. 'Ah, to be young again...' He shook his head in mock regret, then looked down at the paper. 'Abby, it is with the greatest of pleasure that I can confirm your field commission. Congratulations, Group Captain Dame Lennox.'

The Misfits cheered, slapping knees, tables and armchairs to show their approval and Abby smiled her thanks at them, but the King hadn't finished so they stopped fairly quickly.

'Next. Scarlet, darling, I'm awarding you a Distinguished Aviation Medal for your work as an infiltrator to go with your various Crosses and crosspieces and such. Wonderful work, by the way. I very much enjoyed Mr Featherstonehaugh's account of your mission, but I would love it if you would grace us with your presence at dinner one evening, so you can tell me about it in your own words.'

'Of course, sir, I'd be delighted!'

The King nodded, then searched out and found Wendy. 'Aviator Lieutenant Llewellyn, I've got a Distinguished Aviation Medal for you too for your contribution to the abilities of the squadron to carry out their task. It is accompanied by a request from the Defence Ministry to head your own experimental weapon department.'

Wendy inclined her head. 'Thank you, Your Majesty, for the medal that is, but I'm going to have to decline the Ministry's invitation.' She leaned back on the sofa that she was sharing with Owen and put her arm around her husband. 'I've found my place and purpose in life with the Misfits and I can always develop weapons while I'm with them.'

'I told them you would say something like that, but they asked me to try anyway. You will, of course, continue to send them updates on your innovations, please?'

'Yes, sir.'

'Good.' The King smiled at her, then turned his eyes on Mac. A brief frown creased his brow when he saw that the Scotsman didn't seem to be paying much attention to the proceedings. 'Aviator Lieutenant MacShane, sterling work foiling the Prussian saboteurs. I know that it won't do anything to assuage your sorrow at your loss, but you have been awarded a Distinguished Aviation Cross for your exemplary actions and bravery. Congratulations.'

Mac said nothing but just nodded, his eyes barely focusing on his sovereign.

The King frowned again, but didn't comment and instead lifted his head slightly to find the newest member of the squadron, who was sitting painfully upright on a wooden dining chair at the back of the group. 'Aviator Sergeant Arrowsmith receives my commission and is hereby promoted to Aerial Officer.'

If anything, Chastity managed to sit up even straighter. 'Thank you, Your Majesty.'

'You are most welcome, Officer Arrowsmith. Quite apart from the fact that you scored more victories in Muscovy than any of your fellow pilots, except for Group Captain Lennox, of course... Oh, that reminds me.' Something occurred to the King and he broke off speaking to Chastity to search out Scarlet once more. 'Sir Douglas says that you can't paint the kills from that raid on your aircraft because they're not air victories, the same as aircraft shot when on the ground.' He grinned. 'I tried to persuade him differently, but he wasn't having it, sorry. Perhaps you can get him to change his mind this evening.'

Scarlet winked lasciviously. 'I'll give it my best shot, sir; I want those crosses!'

The King laughed, then looked around the group, frowning in concentration. 'Now, where was I?' His eyes met those of Chastity. 'Ah, yes. Apologies, Officer Arrowsmith for being so scatterbrained. Well, as I was saying, quite apart from the fact that you more than deserve the promotion for your exemplary skill as a pilot, I like my Misfits properly dressed as officers when they come to visit me! Just ask Gwen and Kitty.'

He gave Chastity a wink, which shocked her more than the unexpected promotion, before turning his attention to Gwen. 'And last, but not least: Aerial Officer Stone, you're promoted to Aviator Lieutenant.'

Gwen blinked at him in surprise. 'Why, Your Majesty? I haven't done anything more than anyone else and far less than most.' She shot a quick glance at her fellow pilots, expecting to find at least resentment, if not anger, for what, in her opinion, was an unwarranted promotion, but all she saw were smiles.

'You underestimate yourself, Miss Stone. Has nobody ever informed you of that fact?'

Gwen blushed. 'Once or twice, sir.'

'And I suspect they will most likely continue to do so until you accept how important you are to this squadron and by extension the war effort. I suggest you assimilate that fact *now*, because it will make things easier for you further down the road when I have to reward you for doing something *truly* important!'

He grinned widely and the Misfits laughed, but Gwen found it hard to even force a smile, certain that she didn't want such expectations heaped on her. 'I will try, sir.'

'Excellent.' He held up the piece of paper with the list of awards and the Marshal took it from him. 'Unfortunately, that's the pleasant stuff out of the way and now we have to get back to that odious man, Cummerbund. Yesterday evening he announced that he would be speaking to the house at noon today on a matter of national importance. My spies in his camp told me that he was going to use the news of the destruction of Murmansk to push for the Misfits to be disbanded and myself completely removed as the last word of British tactics. The only way that I could think of to take the wind out of his sails was to have you here and pray that you received a good reception. Thankfully, you did and, as you saw, there was no way he could speak out against you after such a demonstration of your popularity.'

'You know, it would have been far easier just to kill him.' Scarlet grinned. 'I could do it for you in a jiffy if you'd like...'

Her comment brought laughs from everyone, but Gwen wasn't sure if it was entirely a joke; sometimes the Irishwoman was a little too bloodthirsty for her own good and she certainly had the training and expertise needed to carry out such an assassination.

The King grinned. 'I must say that's tempting, Scarlet, darling, but no, thank you; what you've all done today will take the wind out of his sails and give us some breathing room for at least a few weeks. Now he'll have to find some other excuse to oust me.'

'I don't think he'll have much problem in doing that.' Abby said. 'It's not as if there aren't setbacks every day in every war.'

'Unfortunately, I think you're right.' The King smiled. 'Which is why I've decided to fund a little exhibition in the Crystal Palace over the Midwinter holidays. If you have no objections, I'm going to put a couple of your aircraft on display, along with some of the photographs that we have of you, both from over the summer and Muscovy.'

Abby nodded reluctantly. 'If you think that's a good idea, sir.'

'I do.' The King nodded earnestly. 'Anything we can do to keep you in the hearts and minds of the people is a good thing.'

'You said a couple of aircraft, sir,' said Owen. 'Would you mind my asking which ones you had in mind? It's just that some of them are too large even for the Palace and I'm sure Charles would agree with me that we would rather not have Bloodhound or Vulture exposed to too much scrutiny.'

'I quite understand and don't worry; I was thinking about a couple of the smaller fighters. I asked Mr Dunne at Hamleys which models were the most popular with the public and he informed me that Wasp has been his top seller for quite a while now, but unfortunately...' He smiled apologetically at Gwen. 'I'm sorry for your loss, Miss Stone.'

Gwen inclined her head in gratitude and the King went on. 'Apparently, the next best sellers after Wasp used to be Dragonfly and Hummingbird, but he says that recently Dove and the two identical aircraft have been selling like hot cakes because people want to get their hands on what are being called "Gwen Stone originals" so I'd quite like to borrow the three of them.'

Again, Gwen shifted uncomfortably in her seat. 'But I didn't design any of those aircraft on my own, they were a joint effort.'

The King shrugged. 'Dunne says that he tries to make that clear whenever he is asked, but nobody takes much notice apparently. It doesn't help that the management of Hamleys made your name prominent on the box and marketed them that way, either.' He turned back to Owen. 'And as for security - there will be an entire regiment of our boys and girls from the Army camped out around the Palace, guarding it night and day, so there's no need to worry about that.'

He looked at Abby. 'Well? What do you say, Group Captain? Will you allow me to borrow a couple of your aircraft?'

CHAPTER 8

Thanks to the King, the Misfits had an entire two weeks leave, almost unheard of in the military, to rest and be with their loved ones over Midwinter.

After the Enlightenment in Britain towards the end of the previous century, there had been some argument as to what to do with the religious festivals that had formed a large part of life for so long. Some people continued to celebrate them, even calling them by their old names, like Lent and Easter, out of habit, but many, in the scientific community especially, had either stopped celebrating them all together or began calling them by the names of the events that were the original reasons for them being on those dates, equinoxes and solstices for example, keeping the celebrations themselves while banishing the contrived reasons for them.

Officially, the period leading up to the winter solstice, previously known as *Christmas*, was now called *Midwinter*, or the *Midwinter Festival*, harking back to Anglo-Saxon pagan traditions documented in the texts which had been found buried beneath Stonehenge some fifty years before.

However, despite the change in name and the removal of the religious aspects, the Midwinter Festival was essentially the same as it ever had been. It remained a time to gather as families, exchange gifts and generally eat too much, and in most households Father Winter still brought presents to children, although, while his message remained the same, his coat of many colours had been replaced by something altogether more astronomical and educational.

Before leaving, the King ordered the Marshall of the Court to organise early lunch for them in the restaurant of the Palace of Westminster and, after stuffing their faces with food that should by all rights have been rationed, the Misfits parted ways, but only after Lady Penelope had extracted a promise from them all to spend New Year's Eve at Bagshot Hall.

Kitty had nowhere to go and no family outside of the Americas, so she very happily accepted Gwen's invitation to join her at the Hawking estate and just after two they boarded a train from Paddington, arriving in Oxford less than an hour later.

Somehow word had gotten out that two Misfit Squadron pilots would be gracing the town with a visit and, despite the fact that Gwen had lived nearby most of her life and gone to university in Oxford, a reception committee of about a hundred people, led by a large contingent of local dignitaries and university representatives, was waiting for them on the platform. Gwen's parents, Harriet and Sheridan Hawking, were also there, standing to one side and looking quite irritated that their family reunion had turned into some kind of circus.

Gwen was just as annoyed to see them as her parents, but she was also amused by the fact that the people had gathered in the part of the platform where the first class carriages let out. They evidently assumed that two such august personages, officers from extremely well-off families, would travel in all possible comfort, not knowing that neither Gwen nor Kitty particularly cared for such things and had gone third class.

Gwen peeked around the side of the door, out of sight in the shadows still. 'Shall we make a break for it? There's an exit just a bit back along the platform.'

Kitty grinned. 'Those people have taken time out of their day to come see the original Gwen Stone. Who are we to disappoint them?'

Gwen growled at her; ever since the King had made his comments about the models on sale in Hamleys, her fellow pilots had been taking any opportunity they could find to poke fun at her.

Unfortunately, though, Kitty had a point. 'Oh, very well. Come on, then, let's get this over with.'

The two pilots stepped out onto the platform and began walking towards the group.

They got three steps before someone noticed them and Gwen staggered to a halt in alarm as the crowd surged towards them, the people in the front rather rudely thrusting aside a man who had just got off the train with them, almost knocking him off his feet in order to get to them.

Gwen found herself completely surrounded, her hand grabbed and shook vigorously by one person after another, jerking her and starting a dull ache injured shoulder. By her side, Kitty didn't fare much better, but while Gwen was overwhelmed, the American was in her element, laughing and smiling at all and sundry.

As the crowd shifted around her, Gwen managed to catch a glimpse of her parents and her mother rolled her eyes and shrugged apologetically, as if to say *it's not our fault*. They had been shoved aside in the rush, just like their fellow passenger and were standing against the wall of the station building, unable to get to them. They were in their mid-forties and Gwen had always thought they looked young for their age, but it seemed that the stress of the war was catching up with them. The lines on her father's forehead were more pronounced than ever and he was looking very tired, but it was the change in her mother that was most shocking; her hair, always so lush, was frizzy and she looked far too thin.

The commotion surrounding the two pilots died down suddenly and Gwen looked around to find that a man had climbed up into the doorway of the carriage behind her. He was portly and grey-haired, with thick gold chains around his neck, denoting some kind of office, and he drew himself up as much as his short stature allowed him.

However, as soon as the man opened his mouth to speak, the whistle of the train blew, drowning out his opening words, then moments later it lurched forwards, sending the man tumbling off balance.

The crowd gasped as one and watched as he fell out of the doorway, on top of some of his subordinates.

'I think they've had enough Gwen Stone for now, don't you?' Gwen took advantage of the distraction to grab Kitty and they slipped out of the crowd. She met the eyes of her parents, jerked her head in the direction of the exit that she had previously mentioned, then rushed off before anyone could notice.

The station let out directly into a parking area, which was deserted except for a single, large, but extremely sporty, white, spring-powered *Panther* autocar.

The family driver, Randolph, was waiting for them by it and he opened the large boot as they hurried up to him.

'Hello, Randolph, this is my friend, Kitty Wright. Kitty, my good friend, Randolph.' Gwen made the introductions as quickly as she could, while still remaining within the bounds of civil behaviour.

'Afternoon, Miss Gwen. Ma'am.' He tipped his black velvet top hat to them before relieving them of their kitbags. He stowed them in the storage space, then, seeing their nervous looks at the station, hurried around to open the door for them.

In his late fifties, Randolph had been on the family staff since before Gwen had been born and had served her paternal grandparents until they had been killed in an autocar accident in Switzerland. He had taught Gwen how to drive when she was twelve, a good five years after she had soloed an aircraft; to the thinking of Gwen's parents, the roads were much more dangerous than the skies, so they had made her wait until she was "old enough".

No sooner were the two pilots settled and the door closed behind them than the opposite door opened and the Hawkings climbed in.

Sheridan Hawking collapsed bonelessly on the seat opposite with a sigh, gave them a quick smile of greeting, then turned away to peer anxiously out of the windows, turning his head this way and that nervously, as if he was looking for something. Gwen frowned at him; such behaviour wasn't at all like him, he was usually far more restrained and composed.

His wife sat next to him, with rather more dignity and spread her skirts neatly about her while smiling at Gwen first, then Kitty. 'Miss Wright, it is lovely to see you again.'

'You too, Mrs Hawking, and thank you for letting me stay.'

She delicately waved away the American's thanks. 'Say nothing of it, my dear; any friend of Gwenevere's is always welcome. And please do call me Harriet.' She clutched at one of the handles over her head as the autocar accelerated strongly, then turned her gaze back on Gwen. 'Gwen, you look wonderful. It seems that life in Misfit Squadron is agreeing with you. And I do so love those coats, by the way.'

'They are rather nice, aren't they?' Gwen smiled down at the black fur coat that the King had graciously allowed Misfit Squadron to add to their uniforms, for the umpteenth time caressing her sleeve and feeling its softness. 'And yes, it really is, Mum. I'm having fun and I've met some wonderful people.' She reached out and took Kitty's in hers.

Despite her poise, Harriet couldn't quite stop gasping out loud but to her credit, she recovered quickly. 'I had prepared separate rooms for you, but perhaps you would prefer...'

Gwen smiled at her mother's reticence. 'We've been sharing a billet for months. It would feel strange to sleep apart.' She turned to Kitty. 'Unless of course...?'

Kitty grinned and shook her head. 'I'm not sure if I could get to sleep without the sound of your snoring serenading me to sleep.'

'I do not snore!'

Harriet laughed gently. 'I'm sorry to tell you this, darling, but you always have, even as a baby.'

They had made it to the outskirts of the city now and, as they headed out into the empty countryside, Sheridan turned round again. 'Right, what have I missed?'

'Gwen's snoring.' Kitty said.

He laughed. 'Ah yes. Terrible racket she used to make. But why are we discussing...' It was his turn to notice that Gwen and Kitty were holding hands, but instead of being even remotely shocked he grinned widely. 'I was wondering why you were looking so happy. Good for you, Gwenevere!' He sighed, looking suddenly wistful. 'I know how lonely it gets sometimes in war. During the first show, back before I met your mother of course, my friend, Willoughby, and I...'

'Yes, dear, we don't need to hear about that now.'

'What?' Sheridan looked at Harriet, wondering why she had interrupted him, then seemed to realise that he had been saying too much and blushed. 'Sorry, it's just I'm really glad to see you back to your old self. I missed you.'

'Thank you, Dad.' Gwen leaned forward and patted him on the knee. 'And you should never be ashamed of anything that makes you happy.' She sat back again and smiled at Kitty. 'I'm not.'

Harriet shifted in her seat, obviously uncomfortable with the topic of conversation, and did her best to change the subject. 'So, do you have any plans for the holidays, darling?'

Gwen's smile faded slightly as she nodded. 'A few, yes. I want to visit the Drakes as soon as our baggage gets here from the Arturo; I have to give them Rudy's personal effects. We were also planning to go to the King's exhibition at the Crystal Palace at some point and we're expected at the Bagshot's for New Year's Eve, but we'll probably end up staying there afterwards until we go back on duty. Oh, and I promised Kitty a tour of the factory at some point, if that's alright?'

Sheridan nodded. 'Of course. In fact, why not tomorrow? We're going in anyway, so we'll show you around ourselves, it'll be like a family outing!' He grinned. 'I'll let Mr Jackson know to expect us.'

'Thank you.' Gwen smiled at the thought of Bill Jackson, the sprightly seventy-year-old man who managed the factory and had put up with Gwen's precociousness with such patience over the years. He had reached retirement age years before, but had seen the war coming and refused to do so until it was over. 'And what about your plans? Are you still having your solstice dinner with the war on?'

For as long as Gwen could remember, the Hawkings had played host to a dinner on the longest night of the year, whenever they were in England. A core of twenty guests from the field of aviation were invited every year and they were supplemented by another twenty or so people from related disciplines. It should, by all rights, have been quite boring with so many learned people in the room, but, because the aviation community was so close-knit, with everybody knowing everyone else, the dinners turned into quite lively affairs most of the time.

'It's a bit harder to get the food, because of the rationing, but yes we are. Which reminds me - I know it's very short notice, but do you think any of your squadron would like to come? Quite a few of our usual crowd are stuck on the continent or have gone over to the wrong side, so there's plenty of room at the table this year for all of them, if you think they'd enjoy themselves.'

'I'm sure they would. I'll contact them, see what they say.'

'Good.' Harriet smiled. 'We've been invited to Bagshot Hall for New Year as well, so if they can't come we'll see them there, but it would be nice to play host to your squadron for once, instead of the other way round.'

Randolph had opened up the Panther on the near-deserted roads and conversation died out as they reached the village of Goring-on-Thames, where the Hawking family had lived for centuries.

To get to the estate they had to pass right by the first and smallest of the Hawking factories. Built in the early 1860's, it was a lovely brick and iron building, designed by the same architects as the Natural History Museum in Oxford, Woodward and Deane. It was very much a local landmark and the huge brass hawk on the roof, the hawk from the Hawking family crest, was kept burnished to a high shine and could be seen for miles around.

Originally, the *Hawking Coach Company* had built luxury railway carriages in their Goring factory, but Gwen's grandparents had been visionaries and had seen that the future lay not on iron rails but in the sky. They had shifted the focus of the company to aviation in 1912, becoming *Hawking Aircraft Manufacturers Limited* just in time to produce aircraft for the First Great War and a new, larger facility had been built in nearby Reading to meet the increased demand from the fledgling Imperial Aviation Corps. However, with the importance of air superiority in the Second Great War even that had become inadequate and the Harridan was now produced at a huge factory near Manchester, which completely dwarfed both of its predecessors. The old Goring factory hadn't been discarded, though; the production line had been completely modernised and, despite its small size, the factory still put together a couple Harridan fighters each day, which were then ferried to squadrons around the country by volunteer pilots - men and women too old to fight, but still able to fly. It also held the design facilities where teams of aeronautical engineers worked incessantly with the Hawkings to improve the Harridan and produce new marks.

Kitty craned her head to look at the factory as they went past, but Randolph had kept up the speed of the autocar, even when they had entered a more populated area, and it was quickly left behind. She soon had something else to look at, though, because less than two miles from the factory, up a gently sloping country lane, were the wrought iron gates of the Hawking estate.

The estate was sprawling, with a fairly large, three-storey, ivy-covered manor on top of the hill and four separate guest cottages set in their own grounds. There was also an aerodrome, only half as big as the one at Bagshot hall but equally well-equipped, a boathouse on the river, some kennels where Harriet kept half a dozen rescued dogs and a small stable holding two elderly horses. It was surrounded by rolling hills and grassy fields, all privately owned by the family, where the horses and dogs could roam freely.

They came to a halt at the end of a long stone driveway and a butler, a tall young man Gwen didn't know, opened the door for them. The two pilots grabbed their kitbags, waving away the butler and the driver with a smile, then followed the Hawkings up the grey stone steps and into the large reception area.

'Dinner is at six. It'll just be us, so no need to dress up.' Sheridan nodded, then disappeared into a room to one side of the entrance - the office in which Gwen's parents dealt with company business.

'It's so good to have you home, darling.' Harriet paused only long enough to kiss Gwen on the cheek and give Kitty a warm smile, before she followed her husband.

The large wooden door closed behind her with a thud that resounded throughout the marble hall and then the two pilots were alone.

Gwen smiled at Kitty. 'Looks like we have an hour to kill before dinner. Would you like to see my room?'

'I'd love to.'

Gwen grabbed her hand and together they climbed the stairs.

Gwen's "room" was actually a suite that occupied half of the top floor at the south end of the building.

Beyond a heavy wooden door, which separated her rooms from the rest of the house was a corridor that ended in a large window looking back towards the town and a golden point of light marking the position of the hawk on the roof of the factory. Three doors led off the corridor, two to the left and one to the right, and Gwen led Kitty straight to the second on the left and through to the bedroom.

Without saying a word, she let her kitbag drop off her shoulder onto the fainting couch by the door, then stomped across the room. She angrily ripped a photograph off the wall next to her bed and unceremoniously dumped it into the waste basket by the vanity table.

She turned, saw Kitty's mystified expression and shrugged. 'I've been wanting to do that ever since I found out about the Barons, but I haven't been home since the war broke out.'

Kitty put her own kitbag next to Gwen's then wandered over and looked down into the basket. Staring up at her from the bottom of it was an all too familiar face. She snorted. 'You have a photo of Gruber beside your bed?'

Gwen shrugged, grinning sheepishly. 'A lot of girls my age probably do. Not all of them had it signed by him personally, though.'

Kitty reached down and grabbed it, then read the legend. 'To...' She squinted. 'I'm fairly sure this says Gwyn.'

She looked at Gwen, who nodded. 'It does. He was too busy flirting with my mother when I asked him to sign it and I didn't want to correct him; I was only seven at the time and a bit awestruck.'

The American rolled her eyes. 'That sounds about right for him.' She went to put it back in the bin, but hesitated, then smiled slowly. 'Actually, do you mind if I keep this?'

Gwen frowned. 'Why on earth would you want to?'

'I'm thinking it would make a good prop for at least one practical joke, if not more.'

Gwen laughed. 'Go ahead, it's all yours. Just don't let me catch you looking longingly at it, though.'

'OK, I'll make sure I do that when you're not around.'

'Oi!' Gwen punched Kitty on the shoulder.

The American laughed as she reeled back. She went back to the door and shoved Gruber's photo into her kitbag, taking the opportunity to shrug out of her overcoat, then looked around, taking in the room properly for the first time. 'It's pink... Why am I not surprised?'

Indeed, the carpet was a deep, lush pink and the wallpaper, what could be seen of it through the newspaper clippings, photographs and sheets of paper covered with sketches and designs, was a nauseating pattern of purples, reds and yet more pink.

Even the bed was covered with pink sheets, pillows and throw cushions and had gauzy pink curtains hanging between the four posts and, predictably, that was where Kitty's gaze finally came to rest. The bed was large, but not quite as big as the one they had shared in The Dorchester months before, so there wouldn't be nearly as much space between the two of them.

'So, is this where we're sleeping?' Kitty smirked, then went and sat on the bed, bouncing up and down to test it. 'I suppose it'll do.'

Gwen smiled coyly. 'Do for what?'

'Sleeping, of course.' Kitty laughed, then bounced one last time, using the impetus to surge back to her feet. She quickly closing the gap between them and wrapped her arms around Gwen, bending down to kiss her.

Gwen allowed herself only a few seconds to enjoy what had quickly become one of her favourite activities, almost as exhilarating as flying and just as satisfying as designing, before pulling back reluctantly. 'Come on, I'll give you the thrupenny tour, then we have to get ready for dinner; when my father says we don't need to dress up he means dress uniform is enough.'

Gwen took her by the hand and pulled her from the room.

The bathroom next to the bedroom was even more eye-achingly pink than the bedroom and even Gwen winced. 'Maybe I did get a bit carried away with all the pink when I was younger. I don't remember it being quite this bad, though.'

A large clockwork water heater sitting in the corner of the tiled room supplied a shower and an over-sized bath, which Kitty eyed with a sly smile and Gwen laughed. 'Later! But only if you behave yourself!'

The final room was a combination lounge, study and library. Almost twice as large as the bedroom, it had one wall covered in bookshelves, a desk in front of a large picture window and some furniture grouped around a small fireplace. In stark contrast to the other rooms, it was soberly decorated, with wood panelling, dark green carpet and a few aviation-inspired paintings.

Kitty immediately went over to the window and gazed out at the countryside. 'Wow, this is a view to inspire an artist.'

While the bedroom had looked eastward across rolling hills towards the sunrise, the view from this room was west, down the hill towards the river. The sun had set a short while before and the clouds were still displaying shades of pinks that didn't quite rival the bathroom tiles for brightness, but were far more aesthetically pleasing.

There was no sign of war or the busy nearby cities and the only signs of life were the two horses, Dizzy and Bruno, in the bottom field and a pair of fishermen on the opposite bank.

Gwen joined her at the window and they stood shoulder to shoulder, absorbing the feeling of peace imparted by the fading day.

Eventually, though, the colours vanished completely and darkness took over.

They turned away and while Gwen turned on the overhead electric lamp Kitty went over to the bookshelves, curious as to what Gwen would have. 'Wow, you don't exactly believe in light reading, do you? Cayley's "on Aerial Navigation", Coleman's "Manoeuvres", hell, you must have just about every engineering tome ever published here!'

'Most of them. I've also got your grandfather's biography somewhere, along with a first edition of his treatise on the efficiency of wing area versus weight.'

Kitty chuckled. 'Grandfather hates his early papers; seen from today's perspective they come across as almost childish.'

'But they were pioneering!' protested Gwen. 'They paved the way for so much of today's knowledge.'

'I know, but you try telling him that.'

'I hope I get the chance someday.' Gwen smiled. 'Speaking of which - after dinner I'll take you down to my workshop and show you my Zeppelin if you want.'

Kitty grinned. 'I'd love that.'

CHAPTER 9

Gwen didn't particularly like wearing her dress uniform at the best of times, finding it uncomfortable and unwieldy, and she was even more annoyed at having to struggle into it twice that day, having changed out of it for the train journey, but the sight of the new bands on her cuffs almost compensated for the hassle.

She had joined the RAC purely to fight, to kill Prussians in revenge for the death of her husband. She had never sought promotion, never wanted to be an officer and have responsibility for lives apart from her own, but it seemed that fate, or at least the King, had other ideas for her. In four months, ridiculously quickly as these things went, she had gone from a non-commissioned officer, to an officer, and now she was a Lieutenant. She was the same rank as some of the other Misfits who had been with the squadron since its inception and she outranked others, one of whom was Kitty. On hearing the news from the King she had been worried whether it would affect the relationship between the two of them, but it seemed that the American was genuinely happy for her. In fact, an aide of Sir Douglas Pewtall had delivered new insignia for Gwen during lunch at the Palace of Westminster and Kitty had helped unpick the old ones and sew the new ones during the train ride.

At ten minutes to the hour they went downstairs and found the Hawkings sitting in the lounge, sipping cocktails.

Sheridan's eyes lit up when he caught sight of Gwen's arm. 'Gwenevere! Why didn't you tell us you'd been promoted? We would have celebrated. Made an occasion of it!'

Harriet beamed and clapped genteelly. 'Oh, very well done, darling!

'Thank you, Mum,' Gwen smiled, 'but I didn't do anything to deserve this.'

'Nonsense! You're only getting the recognition you merit.' Gwen's mother looked at Kitty. 'Isn't that so, Miss Wright?'

'I believe so, yes.'

Kitty nodded and smiled at Gwen, but Gwen just took a deep breath and shook her head. 'Whether I deserve the promotion or not, I received it by doing my duty, nothing more, and that is not something that warrants congratulations. I don't want a party or anything.'

Harriet nodded reluctantly. 'Then we will just have a toast in your honour for the solstice. Nothing more. Is that acceptable?'

Gwen looked from her parents to the grinning Kitty, hoping to find support, but the American just looked highly amused with the whole situation and Gwen sighed, knowing that she owed her parents at least that much for disappearing from their lives and not letting them know how she was for months. 'Oh, alright. One toast, that's all.'

'Wonderful!' Harriet clapped her hands. 'I shall have to dig up some champagne from somewhere.'

The clock over the mantelpiece struck the hour and Sheridan stood to offer his hand to his wife. 'Shall we?'

The Hawkings went through the doors and into the adjoining dining room as if they were leading a party of dozens instead of just the four of them.

With a grin, Kitty gave Gwen a small bow and mirrored Sheridan's gentlemanly gesture.

Gwen stifled a laugh as she took Kitty's hand and together they paraded after her parents into the large dining room.

Dinner had been pleasant and much more intimate than the huge room and table would seem to allow, with conversation revolving mainly around the catching up that Gwen and her parents needed to do as a family. Kitty wasn't left out by any means, though, as the Hawkings slowly got to know the woman that was making their daughter so happy.

Sheridan and Harriet were spending all available time working on a new variant of the Harridan, which they wanted to have on the production line by the beginning of January, so after dinner, they made their excuses and went back to their study, leaving Gwen and Kitty to find their own entertainment.

There was a mischievous gleam in Kitty's eyes that told Gwen exactly what the American wanted to do, but she wasn't quite ready to retire to the bedroom quite yet and besides, she had promised her a tour of her workshop.

Gwen dug some of her old work coveralls out of a closet for them both and they got changed, then headed out into the garden and wandered along the path behind the house that led towards the aerodrome.

It was pitch black outside, the moon, what there was of it, completely covered by clouds and the lights that usually showed the way off due to blackout regulations. Gwen didn't need to see to find her way, though; she had walked that path so many times that she could do it in her sleep. She had in fact, on one frightening occasion, done so.

The aerodrome was half a mile from the house, through thick forest, along a path that was kept clear by the gardeners. The landing field was large enough for most modern aircraft, although something like Dreadnought would be hard pressed to stop in time, and was flanked by three buildings. The first held a machine shop where the elder Hawkings did their tinkering and the second held the double Harridan that was their personal aircraft. The third and last building was Gwen's, though, and it was larger than the one that her parents shared, mainly because it doubled both as a hangar and her workshop.

Gwen took them unerringly towards the side door of her workshop. It wasn't locked, but she did struggle with the blackout curtains; her parents had installed them in all the buildings after she had left home so she didn't know exactly where the opening in them was. Eventually she found it and, after Kitty was in with her, she made sure they were in place, then turned the lights on.

Once her eyes had adjusted, Gwen scanned the space, looking for signs of interference.

The workshop was a mess, with tools, parts, boxes and papers scattered everywhere.

Just as she'd left it.

'This way.'

Gwen took Kitty to stand on a tiny platform next to the door, not more than a couple of feet wide. It had metal railings on two sides and they had to press their bodies together to fit between them, something that Kitty took full advantage of.

Gwen shook her head in exasperation. 'Hold on to the rail, will you? Not me.'

She turned a handle on the wall vigorously for twenty seconds, winding the spring that powered the elevator, then released the catch. The platform surged into motion and smoothly powered upwards into the rafters of the building. However, it slowed rapidly as the spring ran out of tension and jerked to a halt a couple of feet short of its destination.

When Kitty gave her a questioning look, Gwen raised an eyebrow at her and gave her a cheeky smile. 'You're heavier than you look.'

She laughed when the American glared at her, then climbed up off the platform and onto the catwalk that ran along the centre of the building, thirty feet above the floor.

There was no railing along the walkway and it was no wider than the elevator platform, but Gwen negotiated it with a security due to years of practice. After a few yards she realised Kitty wasn't following her and turned to smirk at her. 'Not afraid of heights are you?'

Kitty growled at this second insult to her in less than a minute, but still gave the walkway an apprehensive look before stepping onto it and following Gwen, wobbling as she walked, looking down at her feet, even though the walkway was easily big enough for her.

Gwen waited for her and when Kitty stopped in front of her and lifted her eyes from the floor to meet hers she grinned and pointed a finger upwards.

Hesitantly, Kitty looked up and growled again when she caught sight of the rail hanging in the shadows just above her, running the length of the catwalk, like on an omnibus. She grabbed it then turned accusing eyes on Gwen.

In reply, Gwen just stuck her tongue out then walked backwards away from her, grinning, before spinning in place and continuing to walk away without grabbing the overhead rail.

The catwalk met another running perpendicular to it in the centre of the building and there Gwen had constructed a circular observation platform, about four yards in diameter. This did have a safety rail around it and Gwen ducked under it, then began peeling back dust-sheets to reveal a two-seater sofa, a small bookshelf and a table with a small clockwork water heater along with mugs, various teas and powdered milk.

Gwen flopped onto the sofa and opened her arms wide in welcome, grinning at Kitty as she closed the last few yards to the platform. 'Welcome to The Nest.'

Kitty planted herself in front of Gwen and glared at her angrily with her arms crossed.

Gwen pouted. 'Don't be like that! After all you're only the second person I've showed this to. My parents don't even know this is here.'

'*Second* person? Is it supposed to make me feel better that I'm not even special enough to be the *only* person who you've brought up here?'

Gwen laughed; Kitty's words might have been harsh, but they had been delivered with a smile and a twinkle in her eye that told her that the woman was pleased, despite the way Gwen had been playing with her. Just as Gwen had known she would be.

'I'm sorry. If I'd got to know you earlier, say ten or twelve years ago, then I might have brought you up here first.' Gwen batted her eyelids. 'Can you ever forgive me?'

'I'll think about it.' Kitty pursed her lips in mock annoyance, then turned to look around the small area. She spotted the bookshelf and wandered over to it.

Unlike the books in Gwen's study in the house, most of which were heavy, leather-bound tomes, these had a more common aspect to them and quite a few of their spines were pink.

'Now that's more like it,' said Kitty peering at them. 'Adventure, romance, issues of New Aviator, more adventure... everything flying related, of course.'

She turned her head to grin at Gwen, who tilted her head in agreement. 'Of course.'

Kitty went back to the sofa and was about to sit down when something occurred to her. 'Hang on, how do your parents not know about this? Surely they would have had to at least provide the sofa?'

Gwen shook her head. 'I built the catwalks and this platform myself.' She laughed at Kitty's disbelieving look. 'I built my first aircraft on my own when I was seven, don't you think I'd know how to use a welding torch and a winch? And as for the sofa, at first I just had cushions, but Rudy hated sitting on the floor when he came up here, so he bought it for me and had it delivered in secret.'

Gwen trailed off, a hitch in her voice at being reminded once more of her childhood friend, lost forever, but she recovered quickly. 'I didn't just build this so that I would have somewhere to rest, though;

it's a good way to get a different perspective on my projects. Take a look.'

She pointed to one of the railings and Kitty went over to it and looked down.

Directly below was a half-completed frame of a small single-springed aircraft.

Gwen stood and joined her. 'I was working on her when I left to go to university. I was stuffing her full of innovations and she was going to be groundbreaking. I kept meaning to come back to finish her, but never got around to it and now I won't.'

'Why not?'

'Because most of those innovations have already gone into the squadron's new machines and I've learnt so much in the last few months with the Misfits that she's completely obsolete anyway. Excalibur is the natural progression of what she would have been.'

Gwen stared at the aircraft for a second. She regretted not completing her; it seemed like a tragedy that she would never come alive, but there was no longer any point whatsoever in doing so and her energies were better spent elsewhere.

She pushed herself away from the railing, putting the machine out of her mind, and went over to the opposite side of the platform. 'Never mind her, though; that is what I wanted to show you tonight.' She pointed across the warehouse.

The catwalks effectively divided the building in four and almost an entire one of those quarters was taken up by wooden crates. However, tucked away behind them was a smooth metal object, which shone silver in the harsh electric lights.

Kitty squinted at it. It looked like a railway carriage or a streamlined *Airsteam* travel trailer like they made back in America and she frowned, wondering if Gwen had branched out into land vehicles at some point in her childhood. Suddenly, though, she smiled as she realised what it was. 'That's the gondola of your Zeppelin, isn't it?'

Gwen grinned. 'Good guess! Want to have a closer look?'

'Love to!'

To get to the gondola they had to wend their way through piles of crates that towered over their heads and Kitty eyed them curiously as they went past. 'What's in all of these?'

'My aircraft. Every one I've ever built.'

'You kept them all?'

'Of course.' Gwen shrugged. 'What else am I going to do with them? Scrap them for parts? I couldn't do that and it's not as if I don't have room for them.'

'You could always sell them. Find them a good home. They're collector's items now I'm sure there must be someone in England who would want an early Gwen Stone. And if you don't want to do that, I'm sure a museum would take at least a few.'

Gwen shook her head. 'I don't need the money and I certainly don't want to become the subject of some museum exhibit.'

'It's too late; you're already the star of the King's exhibition in the Crystal Palace and if you keep going the way you are, there'll be exhibitions about you in all the museums and articles in all the text books in the world.'

Gwen curled her lip at the thought. 'I'd never be able to live up to that.'

'Nobody could, but I'm sure you'll deal with it like my grampa does, with humility and humour.'

'And I'm sure I won't.'

Kitty laughed. 'Alright then, with bad temper and ingratitude.'

Gwen grinned and nodded. 'That sounds more like me.'

They passed between the last few crates and suddenly the gleaming gondola was looming in front of them, taking up most of the space along one of the walls of the building. It had seemed far smaller from the platform than it did close up and Kitty's mouth dropped open as she tried to take it all in.

Fully ten yards long, four or five wide and six yards tall, it was built on two storeys with plenty of room for all of the engineering compartments necessary for the safe running of the engines and management of the gas compartments as well as two bedrooms, a lounge and a dining room. It was little more than a functioning shell at the moment, though, with all the controls and machinery in place, but none of the comforts in place.

Gwen opened the emergency hatch in the side of the cockpit, the main entrance inaccessible with the gondola resting on the floor, and bowed to Kitty with a grin. 'After you, madam.'

Even with it just being little more than bare bones, the Zeppelin's potential was obvious and Kitty was still filled with excitement about their planned world tour as they walked back up to the house. There was one thing puzzling her, though.

'Why the hell did you build a Zeppelin anyway? It's not your usual style at all.'

Gwen smiled. 'It was a school project for sixth-form engineering class. The assignment was to make something that could fly for more than an hour and, because I'd built so many aircraft already, my teacher banned me from just making another. So I branched out a bit.'

'And the rest of it? A gondola that size needs a lot of gas to hold it up, where's the envelope?'

'It's complete, but broken down and in storage in the factory down the road. I didn't have room for it.'

'All that just for a school project... I knew your family was rich, but that's ridiculous!'

'And your family is hard up? Come on, the *Wright Company* is one of the largest aviation corporations in the world, with fingers in more pies than a Cornish baker!'

Kitty laughed. 'Yes, it is rather obscene, but we're not nearly as rich as the Teslas. It's just as well we have the Kitty Hawk Foundation and give so much of it away each year.'

They lapsed into comfortable silence as they crunched up the last few yards of the path to the house.

The feeling of nervousness that had been building up in Gwen on the walk back only increased as they went inside and climbed the stairs and reached a crescendo when they entered the bedroom.

She stood in the middle of the room, not knowing what to say or do and looked at Kitty, suddenly shy for some reason. 'I, uh...'

Kitty was, as ever, completely sure of herself, and she stepped forward with a smile. She reached out and slowly began undoing the buttons down the front of Gwen's coveralls, giving her a meaningful look.

Gwen chuckled, then reached out to do the same.

It didn't take long before the two of them were completely naked, but then Kitty stopped, dropping her hands to her sides and waited for Gwen to make the first move.

Gwen swallowed the lump in her throat and licked lips that were suddenly dry. She had seen Kitty naked before, in the shower or getting changed, had seen the strong limbs, the small, firm breasts, the blonde down between her legs, but never before had she touched her. Never had she taken that last, all-important step.

She reached out and put her hand on Kitty's arm, gently stroking her silky skin.

Kitty chuckled and the sound stuck a chord with Gwen, melting something deep inside her and making all doubt, all hesitation disappear.

CHAPTER 10

Gwen woke up the next morning feeling that the world had completely changed and would never be the same again. She opened her eyes to find Kitty propped on her elbow, watching her and smiled up at her sleepily. 'Morning.'

'Good morning.'

Kitty returned the smile, then leaned down to kiss her, but Gwen pulled back in panic and quickly covered her mouth with her hand.

'Don't! Morning breath!'

Kitty chuckled. 'If suffering your stinky breath is the price I have to pay for a kiss in the mornings, then so be it.'

'Hey!' Gwen protested, but without any real force and she didn't pull back again when the American bent over her once more.

Their lips had barely touched, though, before there was a loud rattling sound and Kitty looked around in alarm. 'What the hell was that?'

Gwen groaned. 'That means that breakfast is in ten minutes.' She pointed at a small circular object above the door. 'My parents installed a buzzer. It saves them having to spend their valuable time coming all the way up here to get me.'

She started to turn away, but Kitty held her back.

'Can't we ignore it and stay here?'

'I'd love to, but we arranged to go around the factory with them today, remember? And if we don't show up they'll just send a maid or the butler to get us.'

Kitty groaned. 'We're never going to get any time to ourselves, are we?'

Gwen reached up and cupped Kitty's cheek. 'Of course we will! When the war is over we'll have all the time in the world.' She sat up just enough to plant a quick kiss on the American's lips, then rolled away and swung her legs out of bed. 'Now come on, we *really* don't want to keep my parents waiting.'

Kitty groaned, but nonetheless got out of bed and followed Gwen across the room to the cupboard where they'd hung their uniforms.

Most of that day was taken up by the visit to the factory. While they were there they had a chat with the Hawkings and their team of designers about the new versions of Harridans that they were bringing out, including a sea-going version, which they had rather unimaginatively dubbed the "Sea Harridan".

The Hawkings also showed them the hydromatic airscrews they had come up with. The innovation of the new airscrew wasn't so much in the shape of the propellers, but rather how they provided variable pitch, something that Gwen hadn't even considered in her work and kicked herself for. Under testing they had provided much improved performance for both Harridans and Spitsteams fitted with the more powerful springs coming out of Rentley-Joyce and the Hawkings generously agreed to deliver a few dozen of them to the Misfits to be fitted to their aircraft.

In return, Gwen and Kitty showed them the designs they had come up with for the new Misfit fighters and shared some of the innovations they had come up with, especially Gwen's mechanism for the folding wings of Excalibur, which the Harridans immediately began to incorporate into the design for the Sea Harridan.

There was no hint of whatever the Hawkings were working on in such secrecy in their private study, though, but Gwen knew better than to ask; the British were well-informed of the dangers of loose lips.

In the afternoon, after a traditional Midwinter lunch in the factory canteen with the rest of the workers, Gwen and Kitty took up a pair of newly-constructed Harridans with the new hydromatic airscrews, ostensibly to try them out, but they didn't miss the opportunity to have some fun and put on a show over Goring, doing aerobatics and dogfighting.

The 22nd December, the day after the visit to the factory, was the solstice and much of it was spent welcoming the arrivals and preparing for the dinner, although Gwen and Kitty did snatch some time for themselves for a walk around the grounds and an afternoon nap.

Many of the Misfits had gone home for the holidays to be with their families, but Bruce, Monty, Derek and Scarlet all came, the Irishwoman bringing Sir Douglas Pewtall with her - by some coincidence it was the most rowdy of the Misfits who were available and their presence at the party turned something that was already usually quite spirited into more like a riot.

That was the end of the excitement for a while, though, and, after the guests and Misfits had departed the next morning, Gwen's mother and father also left; they had been invited to spend a week at Lord Gray's estate on the Yorkshire Dales with a few friends. They asked if Gwen and Kitty would like to go as well, but the pilots politely refused, preferring to stay; except for the butler and a couple of kitchen staff who had gotten the short straw for the holidays that year, they would be alone and were looking forward to having the house and grounds to themselves.

With no orders or schedule to obey and the weather holding fine, they spent much of the following few days going for long walks across the hills or along the river, trying to forget the fact that there was a war on and people were probably fighting at that moment. They were successful most of the time and it helped that the only people they saw the whole time, except for the servants, were the two fishermen who were still camped on the opposite bank and who waved to them every time they passed.

Their baggage finally arrived from the Arturo on the morning of the fourth day and with it came the regimental banner from Muscovy. Gwen wanted to get the visit to the Drake's over as quickly as possible so, after breakfast, she and Kitty took her mother's autocar, a small two seater buggy, the ten miles to the Drake estate at Henley.

Drake's mother and father had been informed of their son's death through diplomatic channels weeks before and had already held his funeral, burying an empty box like so many other parents of pilots. They were taking Rudy's loss stoically, having known that it was a distinct possibility from the moment he had joined the RAC, but they were obviously heartbroken. Seeing Gwen was a reminder of happier times that they didn't need, so she made her excuses as quickly as she decently could and left them to their grief.

The very next day, the clouds darkened, freezing rain set in and it was no longer possible to go on their walks. Instead, they went to Gwen's workshop and Gwen began teaching Kitty about flying and servicing a Zeppelin.

Every night, no matter the weather, they spent in Gwen's rooms, reading, writing, laughing and making love, savouring every moment they had together, knowing that when the holidays were over they weren't likely to have as many chances to be alone.

For a few precious days there had been no war for them, but all too soon reality came crashing back.

It wasn't the barking that disturbed Gwen, because every time the dogs sniffed a fox or cat wandering past they would make sure the entire estate knew it. Rather it was how suddenly the noise coming from the kennels was cut off.

She was instantly awake, her eyes open and searching the darkness of the room, looking for something out of place. She found nothing and was about to dismiss it as her mind, unused to such quiet, creating threats where none existed, when there was a clatter from outside as someone knocked over one of her mother's ornamental milk pails.

Kitty was still breathing deeply beside her and she reached over to shake her. 'Kitty! Wake up!'

All she got in reply was a groan, so she insisted. Harder.

Grumpily, the American came awake. 'What is it? It's dark, let me sleep.'

'Something's wrong.'

Kitty may have been a heavy sleeper, but she was also a warrior and the urgency in Gwen's voice banished all remnants of her lethargy. 'What is it?'

'Someone's outside in the garden.' Gwen slid out of bed and padded across to the window. She opened the curtains a crack and peered out, but there was not enough light to see anything, so she just let them fall back into place and made her way back to the bed. She twisted the knob to turn up the gas lamp by the bed there was just enough light to see by, then bent and grabbed her work coveralls from where they had been discarded in the throes of passion.

'Are you sure it's not just an animal?' asked Kitty.

There was a muffled crunch, then a soft tinkling noise as a window broke.

'Pretty sure.'

Kitty chuckled softly, then began pulling on her own coveralls. 'So, what's the plan? Are there weapons in the house?'

'I have a small clockwork pistol in my desk, but my parents have proper guns downstairs, in a locker by the back door. I have the key.'

'It's too risky to go for that.' Kitty stood up and followed Gwen out of the room and across the corridor to the study. 'Why don't we just stay in your rooms and lock the outer door; if they're burglars they might just stay downstairs and rob the silver.'

'That sounds like a good idea.' Even as she said it, though, something, a memory, made vague with sleep, made it feel like the wrong decision. 'The dogs.'

'What about them?'

'They silenced them. I don't think burglars would have done that.'

'So if they're not burglars, who are they? What do they want?'

'I have no idea, but I don't think we should wait around for them to come to us.' Gwen grabbed her pistol from the drawer, along with a box of projectiles and stuffed them into the thigh pockets of her coveralls. The clockwork gun was much less lethal than the one used by the Prussian agent to kill Mac's girlfriend in Vaenga, useless for much more than target practice, but it would have to do until they got downstairs. 'No talking from now on, alright? And no lights. We'll hold hands to keep in contact with each other and if either of us sees something we give a tug.'

'OK.'

Gwen took Kitty's hand, then extinguished the lamp and led the way back out.

The door that separated Gwen's rooms from the rest of the house was open and they tiptoed through it on bare feet and out onto the landing at the top of the main stairs, overlooking the main entrance hall.

They leaned over the banister, peering into the darkness, straining their eyes and ears to try to make out some sign of the intruders.

Using the gas lamp to find their way round their rooms had damaged their night vision and that almost proved to be a fatal mistake, because the two men were almost at the top of the stairs when their eyes adjusted enough to see the faint light they were carrying.

Their clasped hands tightened until the grip they had on each other was almost painful as they pushed themselves away from the banisters in a panic and scurried back into Gwen's rooms.

It was too late, though, and the men called out as they saw them run.

A chill shot through Gwen's body at the sound of their voices; the shout hadn't been in English, but in *Prussian* - they were in more trouble than they had originally thought.

With all need for stealth gone, Gwen slammed the door behind them and shot home the bolt. It was flimsy and wouldn't hold the men for more than a second, but that second would make all the difference.

'Into the study!'

They felt their way along the wall until they found the open doorway and Gwen pushed Kitty through, then stepped back and patted at the wall again. 'Close your eyes!'

Fire bloomed behind Gwen's eyelids as she turned on the bright electric lamps in the hallway, but then the glow was gone as she went into the study and slammed the door behind her, blocking it off. She blinked rapidly, trying to clear them; even though they had been closed, the light had still taken away some of her precious night vision. It had been worth it, though, because the lights would do far more to the Prussians when they came through the outer door.

'Where are you?' Gwen asked.

'Right here.'

Gwen started as something touched her, but immediately realised it was Kitty's hand. She grabbed it, wanting the comfort of knowing that the American was still there with her, but then released it. 'Can find your way to the desk?'

'I think so.'

'Turn the gas lamp up a bit while I deal with the door. Quick as you can.'

Gwen didn't wait for Kitty to acknowledge, but just moved to the left of the door where she knew there would be a chest of drawers. She felt her way around it to the other side of it and leaned on it, trying to shift it. It wouldn't budge, though; not only did the piece of furniture itself weigh a considerable amount, but it also contained hundreds of sheets of heavy draft paper containing every single design and sketch she'd ever made while growing up.

There was a crash as the outside door burst open and then a stream of swearing as the men had their night vision effectively destroyed.

Gwen was out of time. She backed away from the chest of drawers then threw her whole body weight against it, almost blacking out as the impact sent a jolt of agony through her still sore shoulder. The piece of furniture had moved, though, so she growled, steeling herself against the pain and charged it over and over.

Light speared into the dark study from the corridor outside as the door began to open, but it was too late; the chest of drawers was in place and it moved less than an inch before coming up short against the blockage. More swearing in German accompanied the discovery and then the door rattled as the men threw their body weight against it.

The chest of drawers shuddered, but didn't move and Gwen sighed in relief. She rubbed her shoulder, wincing, and called out across the room. 'You found the light yet?'

'Hang on... got it!'

Light blossomed in the room, forcing Gwen to squint against it, but she didn't complain; there was no longer any need for night vision or stealth.

She pulled the gun out of her pocket and placed it on the chest of drawers then began to slot the thin cones into the magazine one by one.

The clockwork pistol was laughable, compared to the kinds of weapons that soldiers had access to. It was extremely underpowered, its projectiles coming out with so little impetus that heavy clothing could significantly reduce their lethality and even a hit to the head at close range wasn't any guarantee of a kill.

It was a fiddly task, but finally the pistol was loaded. All that remained was to wind it and she took the small key from the base of the stock and tried to fit it into the hole in the barrel. Her hand was shaking so much that she couldn't, though, and the more she tried, the more her hand shook and the more frustrated she got. She could feel tears pricking behind her eyes as terror slowly overcame the surge of adrenaline from the chase; she could handle anything in the air without baulking, any danger, any threat, but this...

A hand closed over hers. 'Here, let me.' Kitty took the pistol, finished the job quickly and efficiently, then gave it back to her.

Gwen took a deep breath and smiled at the woman; just that smallest of contact had been enough of a calming influence for her to regain control of herself. 'Thank you.'

A moment's silence had them glancing at the door nervously, wondering what the men were doing, but then there was an almighty thump and the chest of drawers jumped forwards an inch. A second collision followed immediately afterwards with the same result and the door opened another inch until there was a gap of about three inches between it and the frame.

In a panic, the two pilots threw their weight against the chest of drawers. They were shaken several more times as the men threw themselves against the door, but it didn't budge any more.

Suddenly, though, the banging stopped again and a heavily-accented, but quite civilised voice called to them. 'Miss Stone, there is no need to be stubborn! We do not want your friend, we just want you. Give yourself up and we will not hurt her.'

Gwen looked at Kitty, but the American immediately scowled at her. 'Don't you even think about it. We're in this together.' She raised her voice so that the Prussians could hear. 'We've called the police. If you want to get away alive, you'd better go now.'

The men behind the door laughed. 'I think not; we cut the lines before we came in!' Suddenly the voice wasn't so friendly. 'Our orders are to take you, Miss Stone, and it does not matter if you or your companion are dead or alive! Do not make this hard on yourself!'

A hand appeared around the door, followed by a tweed suit-covered arm and began groping, trying to find what was blocking the door.

Without hesitation Gwen lifted the pistol and fired.

There was a decidedly unmanly scream and the arm instantly disappeared, leaving behind a tiny smear of blood.

Gwen's shot was answered almost immediately by a thunderous racket and the two women ducked behind the chest of drawers as the door was rocked by impacts, bullets, fired one after another in quick succession.

The noise was deafening and Gwen covered her ears, squeezing tight her eyes, wishing for the nightmare to stop.

Steady hands cupped the side of her head and she looked up to find Kitty crouched in front of her, a confident smile on her face, and once again she found herself in an oasis of calm, swimming in warm blue eyes.

The American bent forwards and kissed her softly, then put her lips close to Gwen's ear so she could hear over the racket. 'This isn't our fate. We're not dying here, Gwen. You and I are part of the sky, that's where we'll die when it's our time.'

Gwen blinked at her as she pulled back, processing her words. While on the surface they might not appear to be the greatest of encouragement, there was something about them that called to something deep inside her and she felt her courage returning. She lifted her head just enough so that she could peer over the top of the chest of drawers. The door was solid oak, almost two inches thick, but even it couldn't withstand the concentrated, short range fire and there were already several splintered holes in it. It wouldn't be long until it was weakened enough for the men to break through and when that happened they would be sitting ducks. If Gwen was going to do something, it had to be before then.

The firing stopped, replaced by the clicking and clacking of guns being reloaded and Gwen surged to her feet. She put her pistol to the gap and pulled the trigger blindly several times.

There was a shout of anger from the other side, but she hadn't prevented the men from finishing their task and the bullets began to hit the door again. Some of them came straight through this time and the window across the room shattered, letting the freezing night air surge in.

Gwen checked the magazine of the pistol. She still had six projectiles left, enough to take care of both men if she could get a clear shot - at such short range she was confident that her aim was good enough to hit something vital, like an eye. The only problem was that, if she had a clear shot, then so would they, and they had much better guns than she did. She only hoped she could take at least one of them down with her and injure the other enough for Kitty to make her escape.

Gwen crouched, gun held at her shoulder, ready to sacrifice herself.

The shooting stopped and was replaced by the sound of splitting wood as one of the men tore at the hole in the door with his bare hands. Gwen popped up, pointing the pistol, but he was standing to one side and she wasn't able to draw a bead on him.

A huge chunk of the door came away and the long barrel of a rifle poked through it and tilted down towards her. The man still remained in cover behind the door, though, and with nothing for her to fire at she just ducked back down. She wrapped her arms around Kitty, trying to shield her as much as possible from the coming storm; the chest of drawers was sturdy but not nearly sturdy enough to stop the bullets.

Without the solid door in the way the noise of the firing was even louder than before, but it wasn't accompanied by any impacts and then, after just a couple of seconds it stopped again.

Cautiously, Gwen uncurled herself from around Kitty and lifted her head.

The rifle barrel was gone from the doorway and the chest of drawers was completely intact - the most recent shots couldn't have been aimed at them.

The silence behind the door went on and on and, absurdly, Gwen considered calling out to the Prussians to ask what they were doing, but, before she could, a different voice to before, a very English voice, called out to them.

'Lieutenant Stone, Officer Wright, are you hurt?'

'Who's that?'

'It's Perkins, ma'am.'

Perkins was the name of the butler that Gwen hadn't recognised. He had apparently joined the staff recently, after the previous one had volunteered for the army and been killed in France.

A spark of hope ignited in Gwen's heart, but she was still wary; it could be a ruse - the man could have been helping the two Prussians. 'Stay where you are, if you please, Perkins!' She hefted her pistol in her hand while she racked her brains to come up with a way to prove that he was on their side.

'I'm glad to see that you don't trust me, ma'am; you shouldn't trust anyone. However, if I were to say the word *Icarus* to you, perhaps it would allay any doubts you might have?'

Gwen grinned at Kitty; she'd forgotten that the squadron had been given a codeword by the King himself when they had been formed, a way for them to recognise British agents if they came in contact with them. Relieved beyond measure, they stood and pushed the chest of drawers out of the way, then opened what was left of the door.

The scene they encountered in the corridor wasn't very pretty.

The two men were lying on the floor in pools of blood which were slowly spreading across the thick brown carpet.

Standing over them was the butler, a heavy pistol held by his side. He drew himself to attention and nodded at Gwen. 'Corporal Perkins, at your service, ma'am.'

'What the hell are you doing serving as a butler, Corporal?'

The man smiled crookedly at Kitty's question before again addressing Gwen as the superior officer present, despite the informal circumstances. 'A week ago Mr Hawking made the Ministry aware that men had been seen lurking around his home and it was suspected he would be the target of industrial espionage by the Prussians. The thinking was that they would try to get to the work he and Mrs Hawking have been doing in the study downstairs and I was put in place to keep an eye on things. Which is why I didn't go with them to Yorkshire. However, I'm beginning to suspect that the real target was yourself all along, ma'am.'

'Whatever the target was, I'm just very glad you were here. Thank you.'

'Just doing my job, ma'am, but you are more than welcome. Now, if you'll excuse me, I need to radio this in, but while I'm at it, why don't I put the kettle on?'

'That would be lovely.'

Gwen gave him the warmest smile she could manage and the man nodded again, then jogged away along the corridor and out of the door.

Gwen wanted nothing more than to follow him and leave the scene in the corridor behind, but her legs were like jelly. She reached out to grab Kitty's hand and pulled her close, both for comfort and because she needed the support to keep her on her feet.

'Do you recognise them?'

Kitty's voice was soft in her ear and Gwen forced herself to look down at the men, swallowing her nausea as she tried to see past all the blood. It wasn't easy, but eventually she recognised them and her eyes widened. 'They're the fishermen from across the river.'

Kitty nodded. 'Right, but not only that, we've seen this one before.'

She pointed at one of the men. He was dressed in an awful tweed suit that was somehow familiar and Gwen frowned as she tried to place it. Eventually, though, she just shook her head.

'He was the man who the crowd almost knocked over at Oxford Station. He was also on the train with us, but I'm not surprised you don't recognise him; he was two seats behind you. I had a good view of him, though, and he stuck in my mind, not just because of his clothes, but because he didn't stop picking his nose the whole way.'

'Lovely.'

Kitty grinned. 'I know! I'm not sure what's worse, that he made me feel sick the whole way up from London, or the fact that he tried to kill us.'

CHAPTER 11

An hour later, four military intelligence agents turned up and, while a couple of them questioned Kitty and Gwen over tea in the lounge downstairs, the other two went up to Gwen's rooms to secure the weapons. One of them was sent hurrying off to the camp site on the other side of the river, though, when the Misfits revealed that the two men had been posing as fishermen.

It was almost five in the morning before the agents left and then it was just them and Perkins again. He had done a sweep of the house and grounds, checking on the dogs, who had been drugged but were fine, then roused a maid out of the servant's quarters and told her to prepare one of the guest bedrooms, rightly assuming that they wouldn't want to go back up to Gwen's rooms that night. Not that they could anyway; they had been left as they were and cordoned off for a forensic team to go over when they arrived from London.

Gwen didn't think she would be able to sleep, but almost as soon as she lay down in Kitty's arms she fell unconscious as exhaustion and shock caught up with her.

They woke just before midday and dressed slowly. Gwen found that the whole of the right side of her body was bruised and battered from where she had flung it against the chest of drawers and her left shoulder, the one she had dislocated in Muscovy, was a constant ache. She took a couple of willow bark pills for the pain and then ignored it, wanting to get downstairs and find out what was happening.

There was a military intelligence officer, Major Dillingham, a young man with a quiet but intense manner, waiting for them downstairs and he spoke to them at the dining table while they were ravenously devouring a late breakfast of bacon sarnies.

'We have no idea who the Prussian who followed you from London is, but the other matches the description Mr Hawking gave of the man he spotted lurking around. We found a codebook, some notes in German and a shortwave radio capable of reaching the continent in their campsite on the far bank of the river, all of which are already on their way to Whitehall for analysis.' He looked back and forth between the two pilots as he took a deep breath, as if hesitant to continue, and if anything his voice was even more serious when he did. 'We also found a book of photographs of all you Misfit Squadron pilots. My schoolboy German isn't up to much, but one of my men told me that the instructions with the pictures were very clear, that all Prussian agents in England are to kill you if given a safe opportunity to do so, but that Group Captain Lennox and yourself, Lieutenant Stone, are to be executed on sight *at all cost*. I believe it was your appearance and that order which caused our lurker to abandon whatever stealthy plans he'd made to get into the study downstairs in favour of a more direct approach that would kill two birds with one stone, so to speak.'

They groaned at his turn of phrase and he grinned. 'Right then, now we have to decide what to do with you. The King has sent orders for you to be protected and you've got two options. We either post a contingent of guards here to be with you around the clock, or you go to Bagshot Hall, where security is already in place. Lord and Lady Bagshot have been apprised of the situation and are more than happy to have you turn up earlier than planned.'

Gwen exchanged a resigned look with Kitty. They knew that, whichever option they chose, their alone time was over, but perhaps at Bagshot Hall they would be left more to their own devices. She sighed and turned back to the man. 'We'll go to Bagshot.'

'Good! I'll arrange for a military escort.'

'Is that really necessary?'

'I'm afraid so; we have no idea how many agents the Prussians have in England and there might be more nearby, waiting to see whether the first two were successful or not.'

Kitty frowned. 'Are our friends in danger as well?'

'Probably not; we don't believe that the Misfits, annoying as you are to the enemy, are a priority target, no matter the photographs. In your case it's most likely that the Prussians were taking advantage of the fact that they already had assets in place and we doubt that they have anybody in position to make an attempt on the others. Don't worry, though, we're not discarding the threat entirely - we've contacted the rest of your squadron and Group Captain Lennox has been put under guard.'

Gwen smiled, relieved. 'Thank you.'

'Just doing our job, ma'am.' The man returned her smile. 'Well, if you let Perkins know what you want packed, he'll get it for you; can't have you traipsing around those rooms until we're finished with them, sorry. Oh, and don't worry, we'll clean up once we're done and leave everything as it was, although your parents might have to foot the bill for a new carpet; I doubt if the Ministry will want to pay for that.'

Gwen grinned. 'I don't think my parents will be too worried about that, after all they can put it in "expenses" and charge it to the King.'

The man laughed, then stood. 'I'll go and make the arrangements.' He began to walk away, but turned back when something occurred to him. 'By the way, bloody good show holding them off for as long as you did. Corporal Perkins is impressed and believe me, he doesn't impress easily.'

It was Kitty's turn to grin. 'Thank goodness for basic training.'

'Yes. Basic training...' The man blinked at her, not quite sure if she was being serious or not. 'If only basic training imparted the courage and initiative that you two displayed last night; this war would have been over by now.' He gave them one last nod, then disappeared out the door.

The trip to Bagshot Hall took less than half an hour at the breakneck speed the small convoy of Ministry autocars went at.

They were met on the steps of the mansion by Lord Basil "Biffy" Bagshot and three servants, who began taking the baggage inside. His usual wide smile was somewhat subdued, his worry for them showing, but they barely saw it as their eyes had been drawn immediately upwards to where a bright blue aircraft with a golden belly and pink nose was wheeling around the sky, tumbling and turning in a remarkable series of incredibly complicated and sharp aerobatics.

Gwen shaded her eyes and squinted at it, wishing that her bags and her flight helmet hadn't already been taken inside so that she could use the lenses to see it better. However, even without them she could see that the pilot was remarkable and the aircraft was handling incredibly.

'Who the hell is that? And what's that machine?'

A genuine smile broke out on Lord Bagshot's face. 'That, ladies, is *Kingfisher*. She was completed a month ago. As for the pilot, I'll give you one guess.'

'Penny? Really?'

He laughed at Kitty's incredulity. 'She told you she'd fly again. Didn't take her long, did it?'

'No it bloody well didn't!' Gwen couldn't believe it either, but not because she hadn't expected Penny to be back in the air, rather the manoeuvres that the aircraft were carrying out spoke of a coordination that few pilots had, let alone one that had lost both her legs only months before.

The three watched the aircraft, but its gambolling soon took it out of sight behind the mansion.

'She's only just gone up and she'll be up there until her spring tension runs out, so why don't we get you two sorted in the meantime? I've had your old room aired out for you.' Lord Bagshot gestured to the mansion, then led them inside and up the main staircase.

'By the way, I heard about your shootout last night. Jolly good show! You really showed those Prussians what for!' He grinned at Gwen. 'Remind me not to challenge you to a duel anytime soon. Oh, and if you'd like to go hunting some time, I'd be delighted; the bag would certainly be a lot bigger if I took you along!'

Gwen shook her head with a wry smile. 'I'm not a hunter, sorry, I only shoot paper.'

Lord Bagshot's face fell slightly, but he covered his disappointment well. 'Oh, well, each to their own, I suppose.'

They got to the top of the stairs and turned onto the long corridor heading towards the wing of the house that the Misfits had been given as their quarters.

'So, how was Russia? I've heard a fair amount about your work there through official channels, but I haven't had a chance to talk to any of you about it. Was it as cold as they say it is?'

'And then some!' Kitty laughed. 'It wasn't so bad with these snazzy new coats, though.'

Lord Bagshot eyed the black fur appreciatively as the American gave it a flourish. 'I don't approve of fur usually, but that is very nice.'

Gwen nodded. 'It was necessary as well; the RAC greatcoats we were issued with before we went were completely inadequate, especially when the weather really started to get bad.'

They reached the room Gwen and Kitty shared and Lord Bagshot opened the door for them. 'Well, I'm sure that you'll regale us with some stories later, perhaps over elevenses when Penny gets back?'

'We'd be delighted.'

'Wonderful! And welcome back to Bagshot!' He gave them a last smile and a small bow, then left them to settle in.

Rather than waiting for Penny to show up, Kitty and Gwen strolled down the lawn to the airfield to meet her. The was another reason for going, apart from just to see their friend a few minutes earlier, though; the Misfit aircraft had arrived at the same time as their baggage from the Arturo and Kitty wanted to check in on Hawk.

They had expected the airfield to be almost deserted, the majority of the Misfit personnel home for the holidays, but they found the doors to the hangar holding the fighters wide open with what looked like almost the entire complement of fitters working within. Support staff were in evidence as well, moving between the administration buildings, and Gwen was pleased to see a wisp of smoke rising from the mess, promising tea and snacks.

The aircraft were in good shape. Repairs had been completed on the journey from Muscovy and they had been reassembled after their journey by road from Scotland. However, they hadn't been able to give them a fresh coat of paint because most of the garish colours hadn't been available on the Arturo and many of them still had bare metal panels. Fresh stocks had evidently been brought in, though, and the fitters were hard at work returning them to how they were before their hard fight in Muscovy.

While Kitty rushed off to Hawk, Gwen wandered around the rest of the aircraft, nodding to the fitters as she went past. Several of the machines and their respective ground crews were missing of course, away at the King's exhibition, which the Misfits were now forbidden to attend for security reasons. There was no sign of Sergeant Jenkins and her own fitters either and she supposed that they had been farmed out temporarily to a squadron that could actually use them.

She ended her circuit of the hangar next to Dragon and stood contemplating the machine, taking in her vastly altered but, to her eyes, improved lines.

Sergeant Potter noticed her and stopped what he was doing to walk over to her, bobbing his head in greeting.

'What do you think of the changes, Mr Potter?'

The fitter glanced somewhat nervously at the rest of the men and women working on the aircraft and every single one of them looked away, trying to seem too busy to pay attention.

He gave a sigh, shook his head and chuckled at his team's cowardice, then resolutely met Gwen's eyes. 'Sorry, ma'am, but we don't like them. Even though Group Captain Lennox had us paint her the same, she's not Dragonfly anymore, if you know what I mean.'

Gwen gave him a wry smile, trying to let him know that she hadn't taken offence. 'I do, Mr Potter, and I'm sorry, but I believe that it was necessary to make the changes; she's a better aircraft now, which will allow Abby to shoot down even more Prussians than before. I also believe that her spirit is still the same and will be as long as Abby is flying her.'

Potter nodded reluctantly. 'We understand all that, ma'am, but she still doesn't feel right.' He rubbed at his forehead with his thumb. 'I guess we just need to get used to her.'

Gwen smiled. 'I'm sure you will soon enough, Sergeant.'

She nodded at him and the rest of his crew, then wandered off to find a cup of tea in the pilots' ready room while she waited for Kitty.

Kitty was more than happy with how Hawk was and she bounced into the ready room with a huge grin on her face and flopped into the armchair next to Gwen.

Gwen raised an eyebrow at her. 'What are you doing here? I thought you would have taken Hawk up for a test flight.'

'It's very tempting, but I'm on leave. I can wait a few days until we go back on duty.'

Gwen rolled her eyes; none of the Misfits would ever pass up on the opportunity of taking up an aircraft, especially if it had been weeks since they'd last done so. 'Just because I don't have an aircraft to fly, doesn't mean you have to mope about on the ground with me.'

'Are you sure?'

'Of course.' She waved in the direction of the changing room at the back. The Misfits had left their flight gear on the Arturo because there hadn't been space on Dreadnought. It had come with the aircraft and was hanging waiting for them. The flightsuits had even been serviced and the silk lining around the collar, which stopped them chaffing necks that were always in movement, had been replaced. 'Just go already, I know you're dying to.'

Kitty twitched, her body almost out of the seat before her brain caught up. Admirably, she managed to restrain herself, though, and just leaned forward to pour herself a coffee from the pot the steward had brought her as soon as she'd sat down. 'I think I'll wait until Penny gets down and say hello first, but after that don't expect to see me again until it's dark!'

While they sipped their drinks and picked at snacks they spoke about the aircraft in the hangar and Gwen's new design, but it was almost impossible to keep up the conversation because Kitty's eyes darted to the window every few seconds and she wouldn't stop fidgeting.

In the end, Gwen had had enough. 'Kitty, darling. Why don't you go and get changed, then see about putting Hawk on the flight line so that you're ready to go as soon as Penny arrives?'

'OK!'

Gwen laughed as Kitty leapt from her armchair, planted a kiss on her lips, then raced towards the changing room.

Able to relax again, Gwen poured herself another tea and imagined, for about the millionth time, flying Excalibur through and around fluffy white clouds, taking her to her limit and beyond.

Kitty was just finishing her final checks when Kingfisher buzzed the airfield at grass level, did a Split S over the mansion to bring her into the wind, then came directly in to land, not bothering to do a proper circuit.

Gwen calmly finished off her tea then made her way outside, meeting up with Kitty and stood waiting as the aircraft taxied in.

Penny brought her aircraft to a halt, switched off, climbed out of the cockpit, then jumped down from the wing and sauntered over to them. 'Kitty! Gwen! You're here! I'm sorry, I was told you'd arrive this evening, otherwise I would have made sure to be there to greet you.'

'We understand. You had better things to do.' Kitty gestured at Kingfisher with a grin.

'Thank you.' Penny nodded graciously. 'Well? Professional opinions?'

She followed them as they walked around the machine, careful not to get in the way of the fitters as they rewound and checked her.

It was sleek, highly streamlined, with a long nose and a pointed tail. Her wings were rounded though, somewhat reminiscent of those on a

Spitsteam, with blisters for Wendy's cannon, although the guns weren't installed.

Kitty chuckled. 'Well, it's certainly a bit of a departure from your usual style.'

Lady Penelope had always flown twin-springed aircraft, not just in Misfit Squadron, but also in the Schnitzel Cup, competing to see who had the fastest machine in the world. She had never, to their knowledge, designed and built a single-springed aircraft.

Penny shrugged. 'I wanted something I could throw around the sky a bit more, something to challenge me, so that I could make sure I was up to it.' She grinned mischievously. 'That wasn't what I was expecting you to say, though; doesn't she look a bit, I don't know, *familiar* to either of you?'

Gwen frowned and shook her head. 'I...' She started to say no, but bit back her words because there *was* something about the aircraft. The sharply swept-back tailplane, for example, looked very much like one of the features they had played around with, but eventually discarded, when they had designed Sable and Raptor. With that first discovery it was like the floodgates had opened and she quickly spotted other things that they had come up with - Penny had managed to find a way to combine them that none of them had thought of, to create something completely new and much *much* better.

'She's incredible.' Gwen shook her head in wonder, then grinned at Penny. 'Bruce and Monty are going to be pretty damn annoyed; she's much better than their machines!'

'It's kind of you to say so.'

'If only we'd had you in the design room a bit more, I'm sure we could have come up with something truly remarkable for the boys.'

Penny smiled wryly. 'Yes, life is full of if onlys and what ifs, dear, but in the end one has to do the best one can with what life sends one's way.'

Kitty chuckled. 'Well, you certainly have, you look fantastic!'

'She's right.' Gwen nodded enthusiastically. Penelope had been in a lot of pain after her accident, taking strong medicine just to be able to function and unable to remain awake for more than a couple of hours. There had been hope, though; last time they had seen her she had just been fitted with clockwork legs and it seemed that she had more than gotten the hang of them while they'd been away. 'And your flying certainly hasn't been impaired. Are you going to come back to us?'

'That is my plan and I have spoken to Sir Douglas Pewtall about it. He has agreed, but only if I pass my "wings test" again.'

Gwen laughed. 'I don't think you'll have any problems with that, after what we saw you doing.'

'I hope not!' Penny laughed, but then wrapped her arms around herself. 'Well, I'm getting a tad cold standing around out here and I must be getting back to my husband; he does worry so.' She glanced at the waiting Hawk, then turned to Gwen. 'Can I offer you a lift up to the house? Or would you like to take Kingfisher for a spin once she's been rewound?'

Gwen blinked, surprised; usually pilots got very jealous of their personal aircraft, not trusting anyone with them, especially one as new as Lady Penelope's. 'I would love to, if you really don't mind.'

'Of course not, darling.' She reached out and patted Gwen on the arm. 'Just don't go getting any ideas; she's mine!'

CHAPTER 12

Despite there still being a few days left before they were due to report for duty, the rest of the Misfits began to arrive the very next day - none of them was truly comfortable being away from their precious machines for very long, or out of the sky, so they cut short their leave and came back.

As Gwen had feared, there were far fewer chances for Kitty and her to be alone at Bagshot Hall, especially with the other pilots around, but after Scarlet took one look at them, laughed, then moved to a new room, they at least had the nights to themselves.

Abby was the last to arrive, only an hour before the New Year's Eve party was due to begin. She had been called to Windsor Castle to meet with the King and the Misfits rushed out to meet the large black autocar flying Royal colours that brought her, keen to know what their next mission would be.

She climbed out and settled her top hat on her head, the new gold braid of a group captain on it burnished to a high shine, then looked up at them as they loomed above her on the steps of the mansion. 'Was there something you wanted?'

Owen all but growled at her. 'You know bloody well what we want! What did he say?'

'What did *who* say, Squadron Leader Llewellyn?'

The voice was deep, obviously male, and came from the vehicle behind Abby, and she grinned mischievously before stepping to one side.

The King unfolded himself with utmost dignity from the back seat of the Rentley-Joyce autocar, where he'd been hidden by the thick bulkhead. He helped his daughter Elizabeth out, then straightened the RAC uniform he'd donned for the evening in their honour while he raised an eyebrow at Owen, who wilted like a leek left in the sun too long.

Abby somehow managed to keep a straight face. 'I certainly hope you were not referring to the ruler of the Kingdom of Britain as merely "he", Owen.'

Owen smiled apologetically at the King. 'It was the royal he, Your Majesty.'

The King's frown deepened. 'Now you're just making things up to save your arse, Squadron Leader.'

'I am indeed, sir.'

The King held his stare for a beat longer, but then grinned. 'Good man! Wonderful initiative! I'll have to cancel that demotion order.' He started up the stairs towards them. 'Maybe.'

The Misfits laughed at Owen's glum face, even as they made way for the King, followed by a grinning Princess Elizabeth, to go past and into the mansion, all thoughts of possible orders forgotten. At least temporarily.

Over the last couple of days the temperature had dropped considerably and thick clouds had closed in after a brief clear spell. Lord Bagshot had considered hiring the same pavilion that had been set up for the farewell celebration in October, but with the weather threatening he decided to move the party to the ballroom of the mansion. It was crowded, with barely room to swing a dance partner, but none of the men and women of the squadron cared much. While the party was nominally in honour of the change of year, from 1940 to 1941, it was also a reunion - the entire squadron, fitters, service personnel and pilots, were together again for the first time in months. Several of the men and women from Badger Base hadn't come back, though; they had been killed in the nightly Prussian bombings, a few while on duty and a couple more while on leave with their families in London. They were mourned and toasted, but their loss was not dwelled upon, as was the RAC way.

Word had circulated about the meeting at Windsor Castle and consequently there was an air of expectation and anxiety in the ballroom as people wondered whether their reunion would also be their farewell once more. It was becoming increasingly obvious that none of the men and women could relax and properly enjoy the party so, in the end, Abby and the King decided not to wait until midnight to make their announcement and called for silence.

The King climbed up onto the small stage holding the Misfit band, the Individualists, and faced the assembled squadron.

'Good evening, ladies and gentlemen, I hope you had a good rest over the holidays, because your country has need of you again and I'm afraid you are going to have to be at your best for the mission ahead of you.' He took a deep breath and surveyed the faces looking up at him, as if reluctant to continue. 'We have received intelligence that the Prussians will be stepping up their assault on Malta as a prelude to driving us out of North Africa. So, by order of the Ministry for War, the squadron is hereby requested and required to bolster the defence of the islands. You leave on the tenth of January.'

The King's choice of words was telling. It wasn't him ordering them to defend the isolated, but extremely strategically important island, it was Regis Cummerbund, the Minister for War and his cronies. The man had been foiled in trying to disband them, but had done the next best thing - arranged for them to be sent far away and into extreme danger, to a place that had been under siege and continuous attack by the Prussians and their Italian allies for six months already. It would most likely be a far tougher mission than the one to Muscovy.

'Great, another bloody suicide mission.' The men and women in the ballroom had been rendered silent by the announcement, all thoughts of celebration banished, and Mac's venomous comment carried to all of them. Despite the fact that they were all thinking the same thing, they had had the restraint not to say so, but Mac had been drinking heavily for hours and didn't.

There was a stunned hush as everybody held their breath while they waited to see how the King would respond, whether Abby would reprimand him, but it was Bruce who reacted first. 'Buck up, Mac. If we do die, at least we'll die warm this time.'

The silence continued for a couple more seconds, but then Scarlet started sniggering, followed swiftly by Owen and soon the laughter had spread throughout the room.

Gwen kept an eye on the King to see if he had taken offence, but he seemed to have been entertained by Bruce's rejoinder as much as anyone else. She was concerned for Mac, though; his drinking seemed to be getting the better of him and it would lead him into trouble sooner or later - if he'd spoken that way to anybody but the King, Cummerbund for example, then he might well have been out of the Misfits and possibly the RAC entirely.

Abby had taken the King's place on the stage and she held her hands up for silence.

'I know it's not exactly the assignment we were expecting and we were all rather hoping we'd be home for a little while longer, but, like Muscovy, this is where we are needed the most. The difference this time is that we are *all* going. This time we leave nobody behind.'

That news started a pleased buzz throughout the room; the squadron had become a close-knit team at Badger Base and hadn't liked being split up one bit.

'There is one final bit of business before we get down to some serious drinking.' Abby lifted her head to look over the heads of the crowd to a group of people who had been stationed by the French windows. 'Everything ready, Sergeant?'

Gwen followed her gaze, along with everyone else in the ballroom, and with a start recognised the men and women as her own fitters.

'Awaiting your word, ma'am,' Sergeant Jenkins called out.

'The word is given!' At Abby's signal Gwen's fitters drew back the blackout curtains and dimmed the lights in the ballroom.

Nothing could be seen beyond the glass doors; it was pitch black outside, night having fallen a while ago, but then floodlights came on, revealing a gleaming grey and black aircraft sitting on the patio, its pink wingtips polished to a high shine.

Gwen's world narrowed to just her and the machine. She was completely unaware that her legs were carrying her forwards, unaware that the men and women in the ballroom had opened a path in front of her or that they were applauding. She didn't even notice when the doors were opened for her by Sergeant Jenkins and she stepped out into the cold; she was too busy absorbing the lines of the aircraft that she had drawn up plans for on the Arturo, seeing how it loomed over her, so much taller than Wasp, the huge airscrew glinting silver in the harsh electric lights, like a knife ready to cut the air.

She couldn't understand how it was possible for Excalibur to be there; she was supposed to be just a drawing on a piece of paper still. It was like a dream and it wasn't until she reached out to touch the tip of the wing and felt the cold of the metal beneath her fingertips that she knew for sure that it wasn't.

A snowflake settled on her eyelash, startling her, breaking the spell, and when she finally tore her eyes away from the beautiful aircraft she found the King and the pilots grouped up behind her on the patio and the rest of the squadron crowded around the windows.

Every single one of them was grinning. At her.

'I...' She gazed around the group, still in shock, but her eyes narrowed when she realised that Kitty was with grinning as well. 'You knew?'

'Of course! Somebody had to make sure you didn't wander into the wrong building.'

'Everybody knew, Lieutenant.' The King stepped to her side, then turned to gesture at the gathered squadron. 'She's a present from all of us, for bringing back together a squadron that was breaking apart and for giving it the tools it needs to remain true to its raison d'être as one of the primary defenders of this country. She's also very much a present for ourselves and for the people of Britain, because we know that the Kingdom is safer with you flying her.'

Gwen looked from the King to the rest of the pilots, to the men and women behind them, then back to the King. 'Thank you, sir. It's the best present I've ever had.'

'You're more than welcome! Now, do you think we can go back inside? It's bloody freezing out here!'

The King offered Gwen his arm and together they walked across the patio and back into the ballroom.

As Gwen's fitters closed the doors, warmth enveloped them and the King pulled her to a halt and turned her to look back out into the gardens.

The snow was coming down thicker now, settling on the flagstones of the patio and the Duralumin of Excalibur, turning them white in the glow from the spotlight.

'Merry Midwinter, Gwen, and happy hunting.' The King smiled and looked down at her. 'By the way, you're not going to believe who the source of our intelligence on Malta is.'

ABOUT THE AUTHOR

Simon Brading's interest in aviation began when he was very young and at thirteen he joined the RAF section of the Combined Cadet Forces of Dulwich College with the aim of becoming a pilot. However, when he was 18, had reached the rank of Flight Sergeant in the CCF and was trying to get into a University Air Squadron, he was told that his eyesight wasn't good enough to be a pilot, so he had to move onto plan B... something else.

He tried his hand at many things before it occurred to him that he might have a few stories to tell. He never lost his interest in flight, though, and hopes to add a PPL to his very basic and probably extremely expired glider license.

www.simonbrading.co.uk

For news of special offers, upcoming releases, exclusive content, competitions and events, please follow me on social media.

Instagram - @sibrading
Facebook - Simon Brading Author
Tiktok - @SimonBradingAuthor

In addition, souvenirs and merchandise, including T-shirts, badges, stickers and more, are available from the Misfit Squadron store on REDBUBBLE at
https://www.redbubble.com/people/misfitsquadron/shop

ALSO BY SIMON BRADING

The "Displacers" series - a young adult time travel adventure series for all ages.
The Time Traveller's Nephew
The Secret of the Ancients
The Whitechapel Plot
The Price of Greed
The Time for Vengeance

The "Misfit Squadron" Series - a Steampunk series set in an alternate World War 2.
The Battle Over Britain
The Russian Resistance
A Misfit Midwinter
The Lion and the Baron
The Maltese Defence
Tales From the Second Great War
The Siege of Gibraltar
The King's Mission
The Home Front

The Dismal Futures books - stand-alone science fiction tales suitable for adults.
Empath
The Lifeboat at the End of the Universe

The "Twin Ambitions" series - ballet books for children ages 7 and up.
Fight to Dance
Back to Basics

The "Ni Hon - The Two Books" Series - a young adult series set in a dystopian future Japan.
The Black Book

Others
Public Enemy